The Mortality Thief

Mark W. Griffin

CLARET PRESS

Copyright ©Mark Griffin, 2025
The moral right of the author has been asserted.

Cover and Interior Design by Petya Tsankova

ISBN paperback: 978-1-910461-82-2
ISBN ebook: 978-1-910461-83-9

A CIP catalogue record for this book is available from the British Library.

www.claretpress.com

For my family

CHAPTER 1:
Friday

Blood spattered on Luke's face, hands and shirt. There were spots of red on his glasses and a metallic taste in his mouth. Beneath his two fingers he could feel the pulse of the blood, pushing against his pressure. The ambulance was careening around a corner every few seconds.

"It was reported that the patient fell against the concrete supports of a park bench," the paramedic barked to the emergency room team. "The patient is having convulsions that may have caused the fall, so it's difficult to get accurate vital signs. A bystander was able to attend to the wound quickly, and he is holding pressure on the wound now. We understand the patient suffers from PTSD, but we don't have any other health history."

The ambulance had been alternating between the full alert siren and the "hee-haw hee-haw" siren. The inside of the ambulance smelled different from the ones Luke was accustomed to. He tried to put his finger on it. Yes, the fingers, concentrate just on the fingers.

The A&E nurses were fast and focused when the ambulance pulled in.

"I did my best to roll the patient onto his side to avoid a blockage of the airway while respecting the potential for a neck or spine injury in the fall," Luke said as he tried to keep up with the nurses and the stretcher. But he could tell he was losing the attention of the nurses as they watched the patient's vitals.

"Don't mind them, they have what they need from us," the paramedic said, nudging Luke to the side. "That bloke's lucky to be in their care, and even luckier you happened to be on the scene. So, you were an EMT over the pond, were you?"

"I took my training while unemployed for a spell, but that was more than a decade ago. I didn't get to use it much once I got back to work."

A lady in green protective clothing grabbed Luke's left elbow. "This way, please." The paramedic followed Luke and the green lady to a cleaning area.

"And what's full-time work for an American who sits in Hyde Park, I must ask?"

As the nurse peeled off Luke's bloody shirt and started scrubbing everything from the belt up, Luke said, "I'm a specialist working on the Initial Public Offering for British Mutual Insurance. I'm still a little jetlagged – asleep and awake at all the wrong times. So I thought I may as well enjoy the earliest part of the morning while I edited a document." His tone became more clipped. "I need to get back to that straight away."

"Well, my parents are British Mutual Insurance policyholders and I know they're quite looking forward to getting shares from the IPO," the paramedic chimed in.

"So now that I've been exfoliated, do I just go topless out into the world?" Luke joked in the direction of the woman in the scrubs who was now drying him off.

"T-shirts on the shelf over there, sorted by size." It was as if she was asked the question routinely, which she probably was.

"Thank you," he said sincerely as he pulled a red, long-sleeved tee over his head. His thoughts were already back to the world outside the emergency department. "I'll need to grab my backpack out of the ambulance before you charge off on another call," he added to the paramedic.

He got a confused look in return. "Pretty sure it was just you and the patient that got into the ambulance."

Luke's neck muscles tightened as he wondered when he had been separated from his backpack. He grabbed at his pocket and felt the horror where his phone wasn't there either. He felt a tap on his shoulder.

"Mr Smith?" a well-dressed woman inquired politely. "I'm Mrs Mason from Admissions. I understand you treated the patient that came in with the…" she peered down through her reading glasses to a paper, "laceration to right temple."

"Yes, I did."

"We found a couple of Luke Smiths in our Emergency Services database, but none based in London."

"I would show up on an EMT database in the US, but not here."

"We have a very different system here." She started spewing a long description of the National Health Service and the level of public scrutiny its practices were subject to.

He finally interrupted. "What do you put on the form when some random person becomes a first responder?"

She scowled, now both flustered and perturbed. "But you were the first person with emergency training to treat the patient. I will have to get my manager involved."

He groaned as he felt himself being sucked into administrative quicksand.

— · —

The door burst open. The doors of investment banks tend not to do that. And if a door does burst open, it simply won't be for the head of Mergers and Acquisitions. So when it did, Victoria Headley, the head of Silverthorne Staley's Insurance Mergers and Acquisitions looked up, startled.

In front of her was a tall policeman. Beside him was the top man from British Mutual Insurance. Together, the two circled her. She stared up at them in confusion.

To offset the risks to an investor when a company went public and offered stock in its business, there needed to be a granular level of research about the company. And that's where Silverthorne Staley came in. It researched and examined and kicked over the stones to ensure that the investor was getting a price that was fair. At the moment, it was being hired by British Mutual Insurance to prepare all the reports for its initial public offering. Although hired by British Mutual, Silverthorne was independent. Autonomous. Respected. And that's the way Victoria Headley liked it.

The policeman started to introduce himself to Vicky. However, Alaistair Drinkwater, Chief Executive Officer for British Mutual Insurance, cut him off.

He was shouting, his face getting so aggressively close to the woman that the cop shifted his weight in case Drinkwater crossed that very visible line between acceptable aggression and completely fucking not.

"Do you or do you not have the files! Where's Luke Smith! This officer wants him!"

"I've called him, texted him and emailed him," Vicky said assertively. While she stood to face them, she subconsciously eased away. She was remarkably contained given the circumstances. "I'm certain that not answering one's phone is not grounds for arrest."

"You're right!" Drinkwater responded. "It's *you* under arrest for stealing client data from BMI." He grabbed her phone out of her hand. The policeman stepped up, carrying cuffs, while Drinkwater yelled, "Who did you sell it to!?"

As calmly as she could, Vicky announced, "Excuse me, I need to visit the ladies." She lunged forwards, grabbed her handbag off the table and bolted for the toilet, only a few yards from the conference room. She locked herself in a stall and hurriedly sent a text to Luke from her personal phone: "There's a policeman here with Drinkwater to arrest me! You need to

4

find out what they are so paranoid about in that file of death claims. ASAP!"

Then she deleted the message from the sent folder. The policeman started banging on the door. Or maybe it was Alaistair Drinkwater. She quickly logged onto her office email but saw that she'd already been locked out.

She took a deep breath and closed her eyes. *Had she given Luke good advice? Had she put him at risk?* The banging had become shouting. *What on earth was going on here?*

— · —

Six hours later, the staff pushed him out the door. Later, Luke realised he'd been left alone to quietly slip out, solving everyone's problem. Instead, he'd waited patiently, sitting where he'd been told to sit. The room had been airless and hot. He'd tilted his head against the wall and closed his eyes. Jetlag caught up with him and he'd slept, surprisingly well all things considered.

Finally he was shooed out. "If I can't get back to the park to look for my laptop and phone, I'm going to have a blood pressure emergency," Luke muttered to himself. If the backpack and phone were still somehow in Hyde Park, he'd have to call Vicky Headley, the leader of the IPO team, and explain why he'd been completely off the grid for hours and hours.

He refused to even consider if the backpack had been stolen. The fallout would be … unthinkable.

As the bench came into view, Luke saw Jocko, the man who'd been with the patient, still sitting there with the backpack right beside him. Luke sagged with relief. "Your friend is at St. Mary's. He is in good care there," he said as he got closer to Jocko. "His vital signs were stabilising once we got him to the ER."

Luke knew Jocko was a member of a group of veterans who suffered from PTSD. As stressful as this episode would be for anyone, he couldn't imagine what it must be like for some-

5

one with those challenges. Jocko was still very distraught and smelled like he'd slept in a tin of old tuna. But he was an angel of mercy as far as Luke was concerned. "I'm so sorry I've been so long."

Jocko shrugged amiably. Luke reached inside his backpack. Both the phone and the laptop were still there. He could feel his own vital signs returning to normal. "Thank you so much for minding my bag. You have no idea how much that means to me."

"You have no idea what you just did means to that man. And to all of us at the camp." Jocko extended his hand. His look of deepest appreciation and the feel of a calloused hand were things that Luke didn't normally encounter in his financial circles. Both felt good. Pleased grins of mutual appreciation were exchanged.

He wouldn't have minded talking with Jocko, maybe having a walk around the camp, seeing if there was anything he could do – though he doubted there was. First though, he needed to reconnect with his boss at Silverthorne, Vicky. He turned the phone on and read the most recent text. His brow furrowed. He looked at the previous text: "That jerk Drinkwater from British Mutual threatened me. He thinks we stole data. I told him you needed to do a standard check, but he doesn't get that."

He scrolled through the earlier messages that began nearly six hours earlier by asking when he would be in the office, to politely telling him to come in right away, to begging him to call in, to finally demanding he call her immediately. He couldn't believe his eyes.

At the end of the previous day, as part of the standard due diligence in work like this, he'd requested a data file from British Mutual Insurance to check against the death claims calculated from another source. Because they didn't have the time to subdivide the file into what Luke needed and what he didn't, the IT department had sent him the entire file with absolutely all of the information on every death claim, every name, every amount, every personal detail. There was no reason to believe Luke or anyone at Silverthorne would even look at the additional information that the full file contained.

While he held his phone, it vibrated, startling him, and he dropped it on the pavement. That type of vibration indicated a news story on the British Mutual Insurance transaction had just hit the newswire. He picked up the phone and stared in disbelief at the picture of Vicky in handcuffs being led by a policeman. It was clear she was crying.

What had he done to cause this? The guilt was like a punch to the gut.

Then anger invaded every fibre of his mind and body. *She hadn't done anything wrong!*

He scrolled down the article and almost dropped his phone for a second time. There was his own picture! He went back to the text of the article. It said he had stolen data and it supplied a good description: 5'11" with a slender athletic build and green eyes. It even mentioned his most distinguishing feature, his disfigured left ear. The article wrapped up by letting the reader know that he was still at large.

— . —

Manny Chapman's new "work" phone rang, and he smiled. At the end of each of his assignments, in addition to his pay, he was given a new phone to be used for the next assignment. He slid to his feet and slowly pulled himself upright, flexing and stretching his muscles as if warming up for a workout. Time to act.

— . —

Thoughts tumbled like a toddler on a staircase. What should he do? Vicky's last message was clear: they were extremely paranoid about something in the mortality file that he'd been sent last night. BMI management's level of concern implied there must be something either reputationally or financially embarrassing or just plain illegal lurking in the larger data file. Luke's unresponsiveness had obviously caused them to believe that he had stolen the data.

Luke would go to the police. "I can explain," he'd tell them. "There's been a misunderstanding. Here's the file that's causing all the fuss." It was just so bizarre that thievery was the conclusion Drinkwater had drawn. After all, Luke was a statistician. He was the kind of guy who, after leaving the house, went back to make sure he'd locked his front door. He'd never broken any law, driven faster than the speed limit or even lied.

And yet Vicky hadn't said, "Go to the police" but rather, "You need to find out what they are so paranoid about in that file of death claims."

Vicky's reputation would be shattered if he couldn't quickly untangle whatever had just transpired. So would his. This should have been a lucrative gig for him. He needed this, and a few more like it, to get a comfortable retirement.

He stood there, phone in hand, thinking. No matter how this ended, his earning days were probably over. It was a humiliating way to end a respectable career. And in terms of loss income, expensive.

Unless this was nipped in the bud. So no slow grind of police investigation. And absolutely no arrests. It needed to be a news blip, promptly forgotten. For Vicky's sake and his own.

He suddenly realised that Jocko had been staring at him. Luke blinked at him, struggling to explain. "It seems that in my absence people assumed the worst about me," was the best he could do. A note of hurt entered his voice. "I don't know why they would."

Jocko harumphed sympathetically. As if they were somehow in the same boat. Luke had to stop himself from saying, "I'm not like you. I'm a data analyst. I have money. A home. Friends. Family."

Instead, Luke nodded curtly. "Good luck with everything. I've got to go straighten this mess out." And he took off across the park towards his hotel.

He stopped when it came into view. Activity around the entrance of the hotel seemed normal.

He looked up to his room on the nearest corner of the second floor, craning at the window. He saw something get tossed through the air in his room and figures moving. Peering upwards, he realised that a couple of men were ransacking the room. They certainly didn't look like police.

He spun and quickly walked westwards, away from the men tearing his room apart. This day was running the gamut from the good to the bad and was already at the ugly.

He came to another of Hyde Park's entrances and turned in. There was a homeless man sitting on the pavement with a large floppy hat set out for donations. As he hurried past, he realised that the first thing he needed to do was to hide his left ear. He turned around.

"Can I buy your hat?"

The man frowned. "What?"

"Can I buy that hat for twenty quid?" Luke pointed at the hat on the ground.

"For that you can have the shirt off me back!"

Luke considered this. "How 'bout the hat, your jacket and your sunglasses. Forty quid?"

"Man, have I been waiting for you!" he exclaimed. "It's a designer hat, just needs a good dry clean."

"It's an old lady's gardening hat," Luke responded, wondering if the guy was trying to get more than forty. "The hat, the jacket and the sunglasses for forty quid." The man was moving, but slowly. "I need it fast." Luke hoped he hadn't hissed it at him, but this guy had clearly been a sloth in a previous life. The man cocked an eye at him and with no discernible increase in speed, continued.

As Luke quickly put it all on and handed the man the two twenties, the homeless guy added, "I have trainers in case you need to run. They'd fit you."

The hat stank and Luke winced as it settled on his head. "No, thank you," he responded with automatic politeness.

As he considered what to do next, he kept going west on Bayswater Road. Whatever it was, cash couldn't hurt. A couple of blocks on, he saw a Bureau de Change across the street with a sign for an ATM. He crossed, weaving his way between cars, ducked inside the Bureau and put his card into the machine. What was the maximum he could get? He tried for £500.

The machine seemed to be working on his request, but slowly. Very slowly.

For chrissake, when did the world go slo-mo?

A man in a suit entered the Bureau and stood behind Luke. As the door closed behind him, a screech of brakes outside made Luke jerk. The cash machine was now spitting out £20 notes. Just not fast enough.

Another man burst inside. Luke and the businessman both turned, the latter taking a step back until he stood shoulder-to-shoulder with Luke. There was a heartbeat of silence. The newest entrant looked Luke and the businessman up and down. Then he forcibly grabbed the businessman by the upper arm, pushing him back towards the entrance.

The man in the suit managed to say, "Hey! What the ..." before the words cut off abruptly.

Luke saw the gleam of a handgun's barrel against the businessman's midsection. The businessman was dragged out of the door and stuffed into a waiting cab. Luke grabbed his pile of cash. As he stepped outside, he heard the tires squeal again.

The cab had screeched to another stop, about a hundred yards up the road. The man in the suit tumbled out of the cab, onto his face. Then the cab swerved back into traffic again.

Luke quickly ducked into a bakery next door. Standing in

the queue, he panted from shock. His eyes darted around the bakery, his shoulders hunched and his chin sunk.

"How can I help?" The question was bright and breezy. She came into focus.

"Americano," he muttered.

"Size?" The smile she wore was as plastic as the counter-top. He huffed something. She nodded and rang up a large.

He felt his brain slowly coming online. *Wake up and smell the coffee. You're in real danger! You're rocking a tatty red tee and a grubby old lady's gardening hat. The gunman was looking for a businessman and you no longer look like one so the wrong guy got snatched.*

Somehow, this realisation calmed him. *Good one, Einstein,* he told himself, *now that you've figured that you're the one he wanted, perhaps you can figure out what to do next.*

He moved to the end of the counter to stand with a cluster of people, all waiting for a coffee.

He needed to outsmart the guy with the gun. Whoever he was. And whoever hired him. His makeshift disguise had saved him, but he'd been seen.

He grabbed his coffee. This respite had a ticking clock on it.

— · —

"What do you mean it wasn't him?"

"I pulled the guy away from the ATM and into the vehicle. I had the barrel of my gun under his chin and demanded the data. Then I realised his face didn't match the picture you sent, and his left ear looked normal. I was this close to killing the wanker."

"He was definitely at that location precisely when I told you he was there."

"Where is he now?" Manny shot back.

"Give me a sec and I'll tell you." The voice paused for a moment. "Smith is now going straight east on Bayswater Road. Must be in a cab or a bus."

"Go east on Bayswater Road," Manny shouted at his brother Simon, who was driving the taxi.

"I'm sending you the locater pin so you will be able to track him too."

As the call ended, Manny snarled, "Excellent. I'll get the bastard." Then to his brother, "He is ... still going east on Bayswater Road." Manny described the movement of the red dot on his phone screen. "We need to intercept him. Fast!"

— · —

"You okay in there, Constable?" Zofia's husband asked from outside the bathroom door.

"Yes, I think it's over for today. I'm trying to make myself a little more presentable is all. It's safe to come in," she said, putting on a little more blush to compensate for her pale appearance.

"Getting worse, isn't it?" he asked.

"'Fraid so."

"I'm so sorry."

"Well, it *is* actually your fault," she said, with a smile creeping onto her face. "It will run its course and I'll be fine soon enough."

— · —

Whoever was after Luke – and it was certainly not the police – had already tracked him to the Bureau de Change. He immediately turned his phone and laptop to airplane mode and turned off the Wi-Fi. *What else did he have with any sort of chip in it that could be located?* His credit cards certainly had chips in them. As did his badge to get into the Silverthorne office. Plus the hotel key card would. Those chips couldn't be turned off.

He would have to move fast.

There were two eastbound buses stopped right in front of him on Bayswater Road. He stepped onto the 94 and pulled out his phone. He took it off airplane mode, making sure it was roaming. He then sat down momentarily while he jammed his phone between the seat and the side of the bus, trying to make it all look as natural as possible.

Then he immediately stepped off the bus and walked onto the 148 behind it. In a similar way, he stuck his cashless wallet between a seat and the side of the bus before quickly exiting. He crossed the street to the south side, stepped onto the 94 heading west and went to the top level.

The double-decker bus fitted perfectly under the tree branches; the top level was like an amusement park ride. Luke debated his decision to ride up top. There were fewer passengers, but it'd be easy to corner him if someone was still tracking him.

He made a mental note of everything he had: £800 in cash, comfortable shoes, mid-calf socks, jeans and a long-sleeved red t-shirt. He was wearing a large floppy hat, large sunglasses as well as a thin rain jacket that smelled horribly and made him sweat profusely.

In one section of his backpack he had his laptop which held, among other things, a file of BMI death claims data. The laptop had one of those industrial-strength covers intended for use at construction sites. The same section of the backpack held a small fold-up umbrella, two chargers, one for his laptop and one for his phone, now gone. He had a hardcopy of a draft of the BMI IPO marketing deck as well as some mortality summaries, his passport, cheque book, a couple of pens and a highlighter, sticky notes, paper clips and binder clips.

In the front section of his backpack, he had six energy bars, breath mints, a small container of paracetamol, as well as a travelling-sized toothbrush and tube of toothpaste. The outside of his backpack held a half-full water bottle. Earlier in his career, a co-worker had observed that the backpack was prepared for Gilligan's Island and warned him to stay away from three-hour tours on small boats. Luke had grinned back. "Risk manager. Hazard of the profession."

But he had no preparation for this.

Out of nowhere, panic hit him. He'd been on this bus for a long time. Anyone could have seen him. As the bus slowed to another stop, Luke leaped to his feet and thundered down the stairs to get out.

There was an abandoned building on the corner, but no obvious way to slip behind it to hide. He strode past a café with a chalkboard sign advertising a hot breakfast. It made his stomach grumble. As he reached into his bag to get an energy bar, he realised how much traffic there was. He needed to get off that road immediately. At the next opportunity, he turned left. From his previous time in London, he recognised that he was at the northern tip of Ravenscourt Park.

A park had possibilities.

— · —

Alaistair Drinkwater, CEO of British Mutual Insurance, instructed his PA that no one, absolutely no one, could come into his office until further notice. Then he locked the door. He and the Chief Financial Officer Dieter Braun sat at the small table staring at Drinkwater's cell phone, waiting for the call to come in.

"You called him right before Victoria Headley's arrest?" Braun turned it into a statement more than a question. He could barely believe what Drinkwater had done.

Drinkwater barely nodded a yes. But added, "They said they could locate him within minutes, whether he was at his hotel or not."

"Hell of a decision to make," Braun commented neutrally.

"I did some digging after the files went missing this morning. It seems Smith took early retirement but blew through his money too fast. So he came back to work."

Braun continued the thought. "Obviously the man needs money quick and found a way with our data. That's why he scarpered."

Their eyes met in a grim awareness of what that meant. They sat in silence. Waiting.

"When did they say they'd call back?" Braun finally asked.

"They said they'd located him and would be able to get to him in the next few minutes and neutralise him. That was" – Drinkwater glanced at his Rolex – "twenty-eight minutes ago."

"They're probably confirming it's all done and dusted before getting back to you." Braun sounded confident when he was anything but. "Can you describe this provider to me again, please?" He realised he was firing questions at his boss in the middle of a very tense situation.

"My roommate back at boarding school. I trust him like a brother. He rose through the ranks of the armed forces before leaving to start his own private security firm. I asked him to keep an eye on my ex as the divorce was unfolding. Did a top-notch job. I remember he kept saying that his firm did all levels of private intelligence and operations. So I called him to make sure I understood the full range of services." Drinkwater paused. "He assured me then that Smith, and our data file, would never be seen or heard from again."

Drinkwater spared Braun the crucial bit of information – that he had already employed the same range of services to ensure his ex had disappeared after she'd cheated on him.

— · —

Ravenscourt Park had everything Luke needed: trees.

It would be pretty easy to step over the low metal fence and enter the wooded area. He checked ahead of him and behind him before casually stepping over the fence into the woods. The trees weren't too dense, but in hiking terms he was definitely bushwhacking. About twenty feet in, there was a place that was clear enough to sit against the side of a large tree.

He wasn't sure how long he sat there with his head spinning. He was in the middle of London, somehow, left ear and all, until he sorted this all out. His picture was undoubtedly going viral right now.

"THIS IS MY KINGDOM, AND THE DOGS OF HELL WILL DESCEND ON YOU IF YOU DON'T VACATE IMMEDIATELY!" A homeless man, his hair and beard in disarray and his clothes ragged, had come up behind him. The foul smell reached Luke just as the words did.

"I'm leaving your kingdom as quickly as possible." Luke scrambled to his feet. He was back out on the paved path in seconds. As he did so, he realised he'd been sitting beside some casually discarded condoms.

This had more ick factor than a toilet in a bus station.

He walked quickly to the south end of the park and then headed west on King Street. He didn't have a plan. At this point, getting on a plane, or even a bus out of London, would guarantee his capture. If he was lucky, it'd be the police.

At least the pavements were wide. Luke wanted to stay as clear of other pedestrians as possible and avoid eye contact. He noticed an Oxfam charity shop with an eclectic mix of clothes. He was almost past it when he saw something that made him stop: a woman's wig.

He went in, grabbed the wig off its stand and headed straight to the changing room. It covered his ear perfectly, but he looked so ridiculous that he would only draw attention to himself by wearing it. There were some other hats, but none did a better job than his current one. He walked back to the front, put the wig back on its stand and exited without making contact with anyone.

In the next minute he passed another charity shop. At a third one he went inside when he saw the solution in the window – the perfect piece of headwear to cover his ear in a city like London.

He spent ages in the changing room trying to tie it. *It sure would have been nice to have access to the internet for this,* he thought. He guessed it would be easier if he had more hair of his own to anchor it. Eventually he got it to a point where he was comfortable and critically judged himself in the mirror.

Luke grinned, a bitter curl of the lips. It wasn't much but more than he'd have thought possible a few moments earlier. With his deep tan from being outdoors during his semi-retirement and now a turban, he could just about blend in. He could hide in plain sight.

He put his large sunglasses back on, emerged from the changing room and went towards the front of the store. He pictured himself struggling to retie the turban and found a small mirror for sale by the jewellery. Probably too small, but it would have to do. When he got to the register, he put down the mirror and pointed at the turban. The total was eight pounds. He reached inside his pocket and pulled out two bills. One was a ten, so he put it down and walked straight to the door. He hadn't said a word. Even his American accent incriminated him.

There was a new spring in his step. He needed to find a few more things before disappearing. A little further along he noticed the type of shop he desperately needed: a camping gear store.

Outdoor Adventure seemed fairly new. The ceiling was high, it was well lit, and salespeople were milling around the front of the store, anxious to help. He brushed them off, shaking his head and avoiding eye contact. He mentally ran through all the things that were in his pile of camping gear back home. He started with a tarp. No, he'd need two tarps. He grabbed a sleeping bag, a dry bag and then another dry bag, one for the sleeping bag, one for other stuff.

"Where are you off to?" one of the helpful people inquired from behind him. He shrugged and rudely turned his back. "There's a few things on sale at the front of the store, and some great savings if you'd like to sign up for one of our loyalty cards," the salesperson added.

"I'm fine," Luke growled in a tone he hoped would end the conversation.

He threw in some rope, a small spade, a jetboil for boiling water, extra fuel for the jetboil, two sporks, some camp food, two all-weather shirts, a pair of hiking pants whose legs could be zippered off to convert into shorts, two pairs of underwear and a headlamp with extra batteries. He studied the stuff that had rapidly accumulated. "I'm going to need a bigger boat," he muttered to himself. He bought a bigger backpack to carry everything that was currently in his smaller backpack as well as all his new purchases. He uncharacteristically took every plastic bag that was offered to him in the checkout process.

After the purchase, he used the changing room to switch into his new clothes and to repack everything into the new backpack. He stuffed the sleeping bag into one dry bag, the two tarps in the other, and tied them both onto the back of the backpack.

His wad of bills, smaller now, was in his front left pocket, where his wallet would have been. He'd put the receipt from the camping store in his front right pocket. He hadn't wanted to spend an extra second at the counter looking at it. He looked at it now to make sure there wasn't something else he needed before he walked away.

His gaze froze at the very top, on the store's address. *He was in Chiswick!* He used to live in Chiswick. Chiswick was therefore the most logical place for anyone to look for Luke Smith, and therefore *the last place he should be!*

Outside, he spun back on the way he'd come, back to streets that held no record of him.

It was early afternoon and he was famished. He'd finished three energy bars as well as his drink. He knew that if he was being sought by the police, as well as more sinister forces, his picture would circulate quickly. He was increasingly nervous that he had no private place to camp, no place to hide. He needed his own version of the crazy man's kingdom.

There was a bus waiting at a stop right beside him. It'd be easy to hop on and maybe see some camping location options faster than one could on foot. *No*, he told himself, *you need to minimise the number of people you come into contact with.*

When he came upon a small market with beautiful displays of fruit extending out on the pavement, his stomach wouldn't let him walk past. He grabbed some bananas and dates and went inside. The store was small but had a lot of food options in bags and cans that would work for a camper. He grabbed a basket and threw in a big bag of nuts, a couple of drinks, some bottled water, some pita bread and two prepared cups of dry rice with lentils and flavouring in them. He could simply boil some water in his jetboil and add it to one of the cups for his next meal.

The man behind the register may have taken notice of a customer with oversized sunglasses, a turban and a large backpack. Nonetheless, this was a much better place for him to shop than walking the aisles of a larger store. When he left the store, he looked back at it. The tasteful yellow sign said *Medjool Supermarket* on the front, as well as *Middle Eastern* on the side of the store. There was some Arabic text on the awnings as well.

His backpack was significantly heavier now but he felt more confident. He had just started to walk when an unusual sign on a rather large building caught his eye.

Polish Social and Cultural Association.

He looked in the glass doors as he walked past, stopping to read one sign in particular.

BIBLIOTEKA POLSKEIJ, HOURS 10 – 18, PIATEK 10 – 20, ZAMKNIETE W NIEDZIELE

The root of the first word was obviously "library", Luke decided. His eyes slid across the page. Pictures of the inside of a library were down at the bottom. He shook his head at missing the obvious. He then went back to the Polish. He guessed it was open every day except Sunday, but he had no way of asking Google.

He restarted his walk east but stopped almost immediately again. The overwhelming green sign of the *Tekno Bar* next door advertised computers, mobile phones, games and accessories. Also vapes and Western Union. They would buy, sell or repair. Also print or scan. Internet Café was also listed. To top it off, there was also a barber shop.

The Medjool Supermarket, the Polish centre's library and the Tekno Bar were all potentially useful places and all close together, but he needed to find some safe real estate, and soon.

Across the street from the Tekno Bar were the monolithic Hammersmith municipal buildings. What was most interesting though was a map on a sign by the pavement. As he approached the map, he saw the green blob that was Ravenscourt Park. There was a tiny green sliver north of central Hammersmith called Brook Green. It was very small and very narrow and very central. Down at the edge of the Thames River there was a green rectangle. It wasn't large, but it was next to the river and that much more out of the way. It was worth investigating.

— · —

When Drinkwater's phone finally rang, he snatched it off the table and stuck it against his ear. Braun had been hoping to listen in but that wasn't going to happen. Nevertheless, it was obvious that Smith – somehow – had not been neutralised as promised. Drinkwater hung up the phone without a word, picked up a chair and smashed it against the floor. Braun held his arm in front of his face in case there were splinters. Drinkwater kept smashing the chair against the floor, keeping his hold on two of the legs as the chair began to disintegrate.

"Alaistair. Alaistair! ALAISTAIR!" Braun said, a little more loudly each time.

Drinkwater's pace and intensity slowed down. Finally, he stopped.

"I'm sure the odds are still very much in our favour. Let's keep our heads. We're going to have some very important communicating to do right away."

Drinkwater was shouting. "This was the only catch! It was the only possible downside." Veins bulged from his temples. Sweat beaded on his forehead. His gelled hair however remained in place.

— . —

As reports of Vicky's arrest and Smith's heist hit the phones of the IPO team, work stopped and chaos started. Vicky's next-in-command told everyone to go to the conference room just as their access to all of the deal folders on the Silverthorne network was shut down. Everyone's eyes locked on their phones. In other departments around the firm, people stopped their work to follow the story.

Vicky's boss, the partner in charge of investment banking for financial services, arrived on to the floor and walked very quickly to the conference room when he saw the team there.

"First of all, this situation is totally unprecedented and very fluid," he said. "I have just come from an emergency meeting of our executive group and with senior people in legal. We are still trying to understand the charges that have been brought against Vicky and Luke Smith. Protocols are all in place." He was always a thoughtful man, carefully choosing his words. But now the pauses between his sentences were excruciating.

"The deal is totally shut down as of right now and the folders are blocked from anyone's access. All of you will need to leave your laptops out in the work area for security to collect. This goes for all of you whether you are Silverthorne employees, or ..." he hesitated for so long it seemed as if he'd forgotten the name of the law firm and the actuarial consultancy working on the deal, "or on the legal or actuarial side. No one has any access to these files going forward."

He nodded, like they'd just done something fabulous, rather than losing their computers and being blocked from work. "Please be aware that the press will come after anyone they can access who has any knowledge of the deal. The good news is that there is no publicly accessible document that lists members of the team. Management will do everything they can to protect your identities as deal team members. Your friends and family know you've been working on the deal, so the press may find you. Do not make any statement of any kind."

As the silence stretched again, one of the team members finally asked, "Do we know where Vicky is now? Do we know if she's safe?"

"Yes. And thank you for reminding me to address that. She is safe. Our legal team has arranged for her to be held under house arrest. She can stay in her flat with police supervision." Any veneer of calmness in his voice and body language disappeared when the topic of Vicky's safety was brought up. "She can't contact the outside world in any way. Please do not try to reach her. If she somehow is able to contact you, please refuse the contact. It is in no one's best interest at this point."

He was sufficiently agitated to run the sentences together.

"If, somehow, Smith is able to contact you, refuse the contact at once." He paused again, thinking... thinking. "Call the police immediately. And then contact me right away."

He blinked a few times as he considered this outcome for the first time.

— . —

Luke walked straight south on Cromwell Avenue towards the river. It was a long road with few pedestrians and ended in a paved footpath that brought him abruptly to the A4. To his left, he saw there was a long ramp to a pedestrian tunnel under the road. The sign identified this as a subway. The American sandwich chain Subway was one of his favourites, and he'd seen them here in London. He thought of how confusing this would be if a New Yorker was hungry and asked a local where the nearest subway was.

The tunnel had a very unpleasant smell and some graffiti, but otherwise got him to the other side of the motorway safely where he saw the rectangle of green that had looked so hopeful on the map. A sign identified it as Furnivall Gardens. As he stepped into the park, he felt a small glow of achievement.

The park, sandwiched between the motorway and the river, was about twice as long as it was wide. He first walked next to the road to survey the potential shelter provided by the trees and bushes along that edge. The width of the brush varied from about five yards to twenty at its deepest point. The bushes were primarily holly, thick enough to make it difficult to see into, prickly enough to hinder walking into. It'd work, he decided, wading into the widest section of bushes and trees.

Although the bushes were thickest at the edge, there was open space around the trunks. Luke took his backpack off and sat down against the largest tree. He could feel his blood pressure going down. He drank about a quarter of his very large plastic bottle of water, not realising just how thirsty he was until the water touched his throat.

More had changed that day than on any other day in his entire life. He felt like his life had just been tossed into a blender.

His most immediate goal was survival. The gun barrel back at the Bureau de Change was still a vivid image, crystal clear and almost physical as if it had been jammed into him rather than the businessman.

With a relief so intense that it fired endorphins in his brain, he realised he was analysing again. Clearly there was something in the data. He hadn't a clue what it was but you don't arrest Vicky and send a gunman after a data analyst because a seven got flipped for a one, or a three got flipped for an eight. There was something in that data so damaging that it was a wrecking ball going through their lives.

The options didn't look good.

He could go to the police. But he'd first end up in jail as it all got sorted out, assuming that the police could hire in an actuarial statistician to figure out what the data was hiding. And that was making a big assumption. If they couldn't figure it out, he'd be deemed a data thief of stats about mortality. So maybe the sentence wouldn't be too bad. Months and then out on good behaviour, rather than years. But then he'd have a life marred by a criminal record and broken health.

Or he could simply dump the data on the internet and crowdsource the question of what was in the data. But he'd signed a non-disclosure agreement so he'd still end up in jail. He hadn't a clue what kind of sentence he'd get for breaking the NDA but the result would be the same as if he just went to the police himself: criminal sentence, jail, broken health. Without the guarantee that the crowd would solve the problem.

The options seemed almost as menacing as the gun.

If his first goal was thriving – and not merely surviving – then he had to get himself out of this situation. And that required solving the mystery of the file he had on his laptop. I'll be a blender survivor, he decided with almost a laugh.

What was it about this data? It was all so … he paused to find the right word … weird.

He pushed more brush and twigs aside and spread out one of his tarps. He attached the gas canister to the jetboil and started the flame. It was an amazing little device. As the water heated, he pulled out one of his foil bags of camp food and tore open the top. By the smell, he knew it was Pad Thai. He poured the boiling water into the bag and sealed up the top to let it cook as instructed for fifteen minutes.

Luke had backpacked many times so setting up a camp was

familiar and comforting. It was late afternoon, and the best thing to do was not budge for the rest of the day.

— . —

Jocko Watson was cooking burgers for a handful of British military veterans on a small gas-fired grill. He was one of about twenty vets who lived in the "camp", scattered skilfully throughout Hyde Park and the adjacent Green Park. Some had been formally diagnosed with PTSD, others had not. Their rallying cry was better medical treatment for PTSD vets. They had signs at the edge of the camp lamenting the poor medical treatment and financial settlements they'd received and their hope for people's cash donations. The camp was deliberately positioned close to Buckingham Palace, which was good for tourist traffic. The nature of their cause had no doubt helped to establish a working agreement with the police on a host of matters. The police didn't want the negative publicity that came with evicting this group of squatters and were happy to look the other way on minor infractions such as the use of a gas flame. In exchange, the vets made sure there was no need to attract more attention.

Jocko was short, with a large beard that naturally funnelled into a point. He wore a baseball hat with tufts of curly grey hair falling from underneath it. A number of men had remarked that if they could get him to wear a pointed hat, he'd be a perfect gnome.

One of the campers – after reading the burger package's instructions – grumbled that Jocko wasn't leaving the burgers on the grill long enough.

Holding the iron of the panhandle felt just a tiny bit like holding his SA80 machine gun to Jocko. That association, deep in his brain somewhere, was enough to make him more nervous and jumpier than usual.

"Food's cooked fine," Jocko snapped. And slammed the pan

on the ground. "Take it or leave it." He helped himself and stomped off to eat it.

— · —

Luke's Pad Thai was delicious and gone in about sixty seconds. He savoured his last banana. He had one energy bar left for tomorrow. He unrolled his sleeping bag and placed it on top of one end of the tarp. He found a couple of sticks in the woods that might work to prop the other end of the tarp up over his sleeping bag. He would refine the structure tomorrow.

The clothes that he was not wearing went into a plastic bag. He stripped down to his underwear and put those clothes in another plastic bag so that they would not get damp in the night. He didn't put his shirt in the bag so that he could wrap it around one of the bags to form his pillow. It was all pretty neat and tidy.

If his kids could see him now they'd all have a laugh. "Look at this! Camping in central London!"

Within a few minutes, he drifted off to the hum of the motorway, a smile still on his face.

— · —

Manny flicked off the television in disgust before the report on Luke Smith was finished. The side of his fist came down on the empty aluminium can sitting in front of him, steamrolling it flat and scattering tiny drops of energy drink in all directions.

This day had been the most frustrating since he'd left the military. He had always clinically executed each of his contracts. This morning's assignment was the first one he'd not been able to perform in a timely and precise way. Seeing his target's face on TV made it personal.

He'd boarded the 94 Eastbound bus and found Smith's phone. As soon as he saw the way the phone was jammed between the seat and the side of the bus, he knew it had been put there intentionally. With more help from his contact, he had also found the wallet. He was not surprised to see the wallet in a similar position when he boarded the second bus. Smith had figured out quickly that he was being tracked electronically and then sent Manny on a wild goose chase. His best opportunity had been back at the Bureau de Change and somehow, he'd missed him there. He had been within a few feet of having Smith in his hands – and he'd cocked it up!

Manny kicked the table. The crushed drink can went flying. So did the table. It was a stupid kick – vicious – that only hurt himself. It did nothing to appease his rage.

CHAPTER 2:
Saturday

Jocko looked at his watch when he heard footsteps outside his tent. It was 6:15am. This meant that, in all likelihood, the newspaper had just been delivered.

There were many commuters who walked through sections of the park as part of their morning commute. One man, who came by the camp at 6:15 from Tuesday to Saturday, would often leave a newspaper for the homeless military men camping in the park. Jocko loved to grab it first. His fellow campers took the sections apart or tore the stories out, which made Jocko grumpy.

Jocko had been part of the 39th regiment Royal Artillery. He had started to notice symptoms towards the end of his tour in Fallujah, Iraq. In his next tour, in Kandahar, Afghanistan, he found himself barely able to leave his tent one morning. PTSD was prevalent enough that the military officers were quick to recognise his symptoms and to get him into non-combat roles. He was fine with that.

He got a stipend now from the military that was more than enough to live on at the camp, and he sent money to his mother in Manchester when he could.

He snatched the newspaper quickly, looking round to see if anyone else had seen him slipping it inside his tent. Today's headline was worth waking up for.

Rogue Actuary Steals Death Data, Rips Off Homeless Man. The article included a picture of Smith and pointed out that his left ear was deformed. His eyes widened as he read.

Yesterday the BMI IPO transaction took a dramatic turn. An actuary on the Silverthorne deal team was accused of stealing personal data on death claims paid by BMI over past decades. When Silverthorne could not produce the actuary, Luke Smith, or the data, one of their bankers was charged as an accomplice to his theft. Silverthorne would not comment. BMI announced that the deal is on hold.

Meanwhile, the actuary, Luke Smith, is at large. As of 5pm, it was confirmed that BMI would pay a £20,000 reward for information leading to his arrest.

A homeless man, Richard Chilton, claims Smith stole Chilton's begging hat with his last three days of contributions still in the hat. A nearby Boots reported some stolen merchandise. The owner of a computer shop close to Silverthorne's office said a number of laptops had gone missing from a storefront display and they expect compensation immediately. At Heathrow, an Aer Lingus employee reported a man matching Smith's description fled the area when asked for identification.

Police are investigating these and other leads.

There was also an interview with a BMI policyholder in Birmingham.

I've already spent the dividend that BMI said I should expect to get from this deal of theirs, so if this screws that up, I'm going to sue them and Silverthorne.

A beneficiary of a deceased BMI policyholder in Cornwall lamented that she's been visiting the grave of her ex-husband every week, but now she wouldn't have the heart to do it knowing that the details of his most personal moment on earth, his death, had been stolen as though it were a wallet or an iPhone.

He took the paper out to the small group of campers who were now drinking coffee by the group's collection pail. "You're gonna love this one, gents. Finish that coffee and get your camo on. We're now bounty hunters!"

Jocko studied the picture of Smith more closely. *Could it be the same guy who had saved one of them yesterday? Maybe.* If they found him, the payday would be a game-changer for the group. Even the press coverage of them searching for the new public enemy could be a game-changer.

One of them grumbled, "What happened here? Eh? The system works for people like Luke Smith. They occasionally end up on the run but when the coppers catch 'em, no charges get laid. I'll tell you what'll happen. Apologies'll get made. Luke Smith will be found in Costa del Ripoff, get his knuckles rapped and dine out on his adventure of being a bad boy."

Jocko nodded. He could picture that.

Another one chimed in. "Don't matter none. The reward gets paid regardless. We need to be the ones who find the mortality thief."

— . —

The double espresso did wonders for Dieter Braun's sleep-deprivation headache. BMI's IT systems automatically added any new death claims to the historical record at the end of each business day. Back in the day, they had entered specific transactions into BMI's systems to accomplish their goals. A sharp auditor might have caught that, but as Braun expected, their auditors were fast asleep. Maybe 'sharp auditor' is an oxymoron, he thought.

Last night he had manipulated entries in the historical file of deaths, the file that Smith had. Now, if any sort of investigation asked for the historical death file, they would get one with no evidence of those transactions left in it. As CFO, he had all the permissions necessary to make changes to files. But even

BMI's antiquated system automatically generated a report that showed changes had been made to the files last night. That email would go to three people: two members of the IT team and Braun himself. He had another move left in his bag of tricks to cover the only remaining tracks.

He pulled the old stationary bike out of the closet. He couldn't go to the gym. Too many people there knew he was the CFO at BMI. A couple of gym rats were senior management at the London Stock Exchange Group. A month ago, they'd introduced themselves and expressed their pleasure that BMI would be a new listing on the exchange with its completion of the IPO. The dearth of new listings on the London Stock Exchange, together with the transfer away from London to New York of some large stocks, was a bellwether for London's decreasing significance in the financial realm. BMI going public in London was good news for them all.

They'd all nailed that engaged collegiality that never once slid into a schmooze. They were too slick to schmooze.

They'd be looking down their noses at him now. Braun loathed them and what they represented. He knew he was better than all of them – combined. He knew he was smarter and worked harder and paid more attention to more details than they did. But they somehow thought they were his equal or now even his superior. It grated like cheese in an Italian café.

He knew he wouldn't be able to compare his speed on this bike to the bikes at the gym and he knew his mind would wander today. He kept going through all the possible outcomes until he finally stopped pedalling, grabbed a pad of paper and wrote them down.

— · —

The rose that Luke had given her a couple of nights earlier was still on Vicky's nightstand. It helped her remember the evening that seemed so far away now. Her phone and laptop were gone.

She felt totally helpless being cut off from Luke, Silverthorne and her team. She could not browse the internet. She was wearing a GPS bracelet on her ankle.

On waking, it took her a couple of seconds to recall the names of the two policewomen. One was Jane and the other was Fiona. At least one of them would be in her flat at all times.

Her life and career had come crashing down in the last twenty-four hours and she really didn't understand why.

Why didn't the client understand that my team needed to verify data from root source data files to do its job? Why was BMI so worried about Silverthorne having access to the data unless it revealed something they didn't want revealed?

With no need to prepare for work, she lingered in front of the mirror, fluffing her hair and pulling it into new styles. Then she eyed herself critically. *Still good,* she thought. *Damn good,* she amended. Her legs and rear were, perhaps, a little too round and full which, for some reason, looked great on Kim Kardashian. But she didn't like it. At least not on herself. But she didn't have much choice in the matter.

The rest of her body was trim and strong. Her hair was as black as the night, and hopefully that would remain the case for years to come. Her eyes were blue. What a weird combination her parents had bestowed on her. Her mother had described her as "not a conventional beauty but gifted with brains and ambition."

All her brains hadn't helped her see this one coming. And if it wasn't sorted soon, her ambition would be forever stunted. She'd been told that the first hearing was probably a couple of weeks away. An eternity. The only scenario that could speed up resolution would be if Luke found something in the data that changed the situation and came forward with it. If he were arrested before solving that problem, it would be impossible to determine what was in the file.

— . —

Ludicrously, the Simon and Garfunkel song, *Slow Down, You Move Too Fast*, popped into his head and Luke matched his steps to the song's slower beat. He'd already made sure there was nothing he'd need that day in his backpack. He wanted as much room in there as possible to fill with food. He put everything else into the bigger backpack and did his best to hide it under some sticks and brush that he'd pulled together. If he got back and the big backpack was gone, that was a problem. But he was still moving at the brisker pace of *hi-ho hi-ho it's off to work we go*. And that just didn't fit with his new down-and-dirty vibe.

He switched back to Simon and Garfunkel's *Slow Down, You Move to Fast*. "Got to make the morning last," he sang quietly to himself, forcing his feet to match the tune.

He chose dates, bananas and one large mango from the Medjool Market's outdoor stands before turning into the store. On the way in, his eyes were caught by the headline on the newspapers stacked right beside the door. *Banker Robs Widows and Orphans!* In the middle of the front page was his picture with the homeless man's hat photoshopped onto him! He froze like he'd been hit by a sledgehammer.

When he unglued his eyes from the picture, they went to the £20,000 reward for information leading to his capture. Suddenly, he realised that he'd been standing in front of the door to the shop for far too long.

Flustered, Luke started grabbing stuff off the shelves. He felt sweat like a flea crawling from his armpits down to his waist.

Stay calm, he told himself. *Breathe. Make it look like you do this every day.* He paid the total quickly in cash. He avoided eye contact and didn't speak a word. As he left the store, he kicked himself for not buying the paper. He may as well know as much about the search for Luke Smith as possible.

Minimising the total number of people he had exposure

to would have to be one of his top priorities. He had to find a routine that involved as few people as possible. If just the same handful of people saw him regularly, their brains would become less and less likely to focus on him.

At the Polish Centre, he paused and looked through the large glass window. He could see most of the lobby. It was better to spend a half a minute outside orientating himself than to look totally lost when he stepped inside.

Seated behind the reception counter were a man and a woman. He saw a small sign that indicated the library was to the right. There were other signs in Polish pointing to the left. One was clearly for a restaurant and one for a washroom. He couldn't guess the others. People were coming into the building and walking purposefully without even a glance towards the counter. The people behind the counter had their heads down. He would walk in purposefully, as though he did it every day. If either of them looked up at a man in a turban with a backpack, he would just nod. If they spoke to him in English or Polish, he would just point at the sign to the library and keep moving.

As he went through the doors, he noticed he'd inhaled deeply and was holding his breath. Like he was diving in the deep end of a pool. From the corner of his eye, he could see that neither of the people behind the counter even looked up. He made the right turn through a doorway and found himself in a narrow stairway. He felt nervous in such a narrow space, which was unusual for him. He gulped for air. Claustrophobia, it seemed, was in the basket of other anxieties he'd acquired yesterday.

He went through the solid wooden door with the name *Biblioteka* on it and into a surprisingly large library. Most of the room was full of metal shelves of books. There wasn't anyone else in the room and there didn't seem to be any sort of desk or station for a librarian. There was a very long table that ran down the middle of the entire room. He felt like he was back in the seventies or eighties. Retro. So out it's in.

Right against the back wall, an afterthought to the room's layout, were three large, very old desktop computers. Internally, Luke jumped for joy. Anyone in the centre of the room would be able to see the back of a person sitting at the table, but not their face.

Luke walked slowly to the back wall, checking between the aisles for people, but found no one. At one end of the computer table, in the corner of the room, was a window. It was hard to say if anyone could see into that window from another building. In the corner of the room, at the other end of the computer table, was a disabled toilet. When he entered it, he mentally jumped for joy again. The room was large with a very big sink and an oversupply of tissue. He checked his turban in the mirror, and it looked fine. He'd caught some sun yesterday, and his beard was starting to be visible.

As Luke left the washroom, he spotted that the side of each computer had two tiny pieces of paper, stuck there by old, discoloured transparent tape. He looked more closely. One, clearly the most recent, looked like it could be an internet password. The tape over the other piece of paper was faded and had started to peel away from the computer. Presumably, this was a password to use the computer itself. Some characters were readable, others not so much. He recognised a good puzzle when he saw one.

He loved puzzles.

He sat at the computer furthest from the restroom, plugged in the laptop charger and attached it to the laptop. He sighed in relief when the lightning bolt appeared over the battery icon.

He started narrowing the possibilities in the password puzzle. On his third attempt at the password, he had success. As long as no one recognised him while he sat pointed into the corner, using his laptop and the desktop, this was a homerun. Anonymity, power and the internet!

While he'd closed his eyes for a moment in pure relief,

there was that annoying voice in the back of his brain that wouldn't let him just enjoy it. It was saying, eventually they'll notice a Sikh who can't speak Polish using their free computers. How long can this last?

— . —

Manny was dressed the same way as the day before: his loose leather jacket with his 1911 .45 ACP strapped to the small of his back. His four-inch knife was strapped right above his left ankle underneath jeans and above steel-toed boots. He had transparent latex gloves in his jacket pocket next to his sunglasses. He didn't carry any extra weight and he was solid muscle. The boots weren't great for walking or running, but they were very effective for kicking people. He liked the three O's; Overarm, Overreact and Overkill. If he somehow got close enough to Smith to do any of these things today, he'd be ready.

He was no more than one hundred yards into Hyde Park when he heard someone behind him exclaim:

"Sergeant?"

Manny swung around quickly, his mind changing gears.

"Private Jocko Watson, 39th" the man said. "Kandahar!"

"Ah, yes, the glue who kept us all working," Manny said, recovering quickly.

Jocko reached out with both arms expecting a hug. Manny never made bodily contact with anyone when he was dressed for work, so he took a half step back, grabbed Jocko's right hand, and shook it firmly and sincerely. The last thing he needed was someone slapping him on his back when his gun was strapped there.

"What you up to, mate?" Manny asked.

"I'm camping with a bunch of other PTSD vets over by the palace."

"Really!" Manny replied. There was a lot of information in that one sentence. "I read about that," he lied. "How many of you are there?"

"Coupla dozen. Comes and goes."

"The coppers give you grief?"

"Not really. We've worked things out with them. If we feel harassed by anyone, the tabloids are on it pretty quick."

"Good work!" Manny said, genuinely impressed.

"We gotta keep up." Jocko's partner interrupted from a few yards away and Jocko quickly shooed him away. "You carry on. I'll catch up in a sec."

"So, what are you up to today?" Manny asked stepping back and looking up and down at Jocko's fatigues.

"We clean up rubbish in the park. Helps our profile with the police and the public." He stopped himself from wincing at how weak that sounded from one military person to another. "Today we are using that as a cover to search for that data thief. That reward will help our camp a lot."

"Good for you. I read what he did to that beggar. Taking his money and all. What kind of man does that?"

Manny and Jocko did that male thing of shaking their heads in mournful astonishment at the world. *Can you believe what the world coming to. Outrageous.* The words hung in the air, unspoken but loud enough for them to hear.

"I'll let you get back to your search," Manny concluded. "I'll drop over to your camp some time and we'll catch up proper."

"Look forward to that, Sergeant." Jocko had a big smile as he turned and trotted towards his rubbish-collecting partner.

Manny strode off in the opposite direction. He hadn't hated the military; it had frustrated the hell out of him. It wasn't the hurry-up-and-wait combined with life-defining risk. That, and the abysmal pay, had been well advertised. No one had tricked him into signing up. But living it really ground his gears. He went through Kandahar more annoyed than terrified, more irritated with the locals and his superiors than with the war. If he got PTSD it'd be from sheer aggravation.

— · —

Amber Leung stepped through the gate in the fence and onto the grassy field. She was so hopeful this would work out. She wore studs, athletic shorts and a white rugby jersey rescued from the very bottom of her closet. Her hair was tied back. She held a black jersey in one hand and her water jug in the other. She approached a handful of women, most of them older than her, stretching.

"Morning," she said with a smile.

"Morning," came back to her in a British accent as the woman stood and fist-bumped her. "Newbie?"

"Ya. I saw you folks out here two weeks ago and promised myself I would drag my out-of-shape ass out here." She paused as others looked her up and down, with nods. "I'm not new to touch rugby though, played in school in Hong Kong a few years ago. I was hoping I could join you."

"Welcome. I see you've got the idea," the lady said looking at the other jersey in Amber's hand. "We'll let you know if the dark team needs you more than the white team. Only other thing you'll need is twenty quid to help us cover the ref and rent the pitch."

"Got it," Amber said with a smile, pulling some bills out of her pocket. Others were fist-bumping and fiving her now.

"There's a couple of us from Hong Kong. One from Singapore I believe. They'll probably be along real soon," came from a tall blond with an Aussie accent. "It's a regular United Nations here."

"Thank you," Amber said with sincerity.

"I'm Jess, and I'm glad you are thankful now, 'cause if you're that out of shape, you might well be heavin' before we all be leavin'." There were chuckles from the group which was now more than a dozen.

"Wouldn't be the first time," Amber grinned and raised her jug slightly. Amber found a bit of space and started stretching on the ground with the others.

"How'd you get here?" came from a lady whose head was also on the grass, a few feet away from Amber's.

"Work transfer. When the UK opened the door a few years back and offered passports, I jumped at that."

"What do you do?"

"I'm an actuarial student." Amber paused as she switched to a different stretch.

"Heard of that. You do insurance maths and the like, right?"

"Sure do."

"And there's a series of ridiculous tests to make sure you're legit?"

"Oh ya. When you pass all the exams you are referred to as a Fellow."

"Well, you won't be getting on this pitch if you're a fellow."

Amber chuckled. *So far, so good*, she thought.

"On your feet, ladies," was bawled across the group and they all began to stand. "Any more stretching and we'll be ballerinas."

— . —

Luke's mood dampened after his first analysis of the data. He added up the deaths in the last full calendar year and compared the total to what was shown in the financial statements. The number in the financials was a bit smaller. He double-checked how he was doing his maths. He doubled-checked that the field he was totalling was the correct death benefit field. Was there perhaps another field that would sum to the right number? He couldn't seem to find one.

It also occurred to him that he should at least understand what it meant to wear a black turban. He discovered that it was a reminder of British persecution of Sikhs in 1919 and represented humility. From his selfish perspective, black was much better than any other colour as it didn't show the dirt. He was relieved to read that the turban was supposed to cover the top of one's ears. The pictures he saw had the turban going as low on the ear as he was wearing his, just enough to hide the part of his ear that was misshapen. One of the sites noted that Shia Muslims may also wear turbans.

He looked up the sign language hand signal for being mute. He had done well so far keeping his mouth shut, but this might be useful to know. It appeared that making a fist and holding it to one's chin, palm towards the mouth, was the way to do it. Even if he performed it, would anybody understand it?

He did the same maths for the year before last and it didn't add up either. In that year, the total death claims paid according to the file were lower than what was shown in the financials. In both years, the variation wasn't huge, but it certainly wasn't zero.

Luke heard the door to the library open behind him and he instinctively froze. After a half a minute it was clear that it was a group of young girls and boys speaking Polish.

The results for the third year were just like the other years: the actual claims were lower than what was shown in the financials. This was perplexing. However, it was 4:30pm and time to leave. He sighed. He'd planned to have this all sorted out by now.

— . —

Amber said her goodbyes as the other players walked away. She sat and chugged what remained in her water jug. There wasn't much grass underneath her, mostly mud. She didn't care, she was already covered in it. The game was judged to be an "excellent match" by the participants, and it couldn't have been more excellent from Amber's perspective. She was physically exhausted, but the endorphins were pumping and she had that post-game high.

She was moving quickly through the actuarial exams. They were offered every six months and she had just completed one right before the BMI assignment started. The screeching halt to the work on BMI was a huge disappointment, but the silver lining was the unusual break it provided. She had been, as her mother would say, "burning the candle at both ends." She'd been indoors so much her skin was going as translucent as a shrimp's. It would take at least another week before her boss could put her on enough other client projects to fill her plate. Until then, she could alternate studying and playing rugby.

Her inclusion in the BMI IPO team, even as its lowest life form, had been a stroke of good fortune. It was her first exposure to mergers and acquisitions, and to the bankers, lawyers and specialists, such as Luke Smith, who came from various firms to comprise the deal team. Watching Vicky Headley lead the entire deal was the real eye-opener for her. At her boring consulting agency, everything was measured in billed hours of work. But for bankers, the only thing that mattered was whether the deal got over the finish line. Kind of like that try she'd scored towards the end of the match.

Her brief brush with Luke Smith, corrupt and a thief, was wildly exciting. A thief. A corrupt thief. Who had now disappeared. It was the most exciting thing that had ever happened to her. She couldn't help but think about it.

She had always been naturally curious, and her father had supported that. She could hear him saying, "He who asks a question is a fool for five minutes. He who doesn't ask, is a fool forever."

She knew Luke Smith had written a number of articles and papers on how to judge the amount of variation in mortality results. Those would be easy to find. There was no better indication of what someone had been focused on than what they had written about. She would put herself in Luke's shoes and go as far into his head as possible ... see what she could find.

She wondered how long she had been sitting there in the muddy grass. Her best ideas always came when she was as far out of her routine as possible. Like right now.

— · —

"No confirmed sightings yet that we're aware of," the BBC reporter said. The *New Scotland Yard* sign could be seen clearly in the background of the interview. "Police have received a continuous stream of calls, texts and pictures as people have identified suspects but none have been confirmed. There have also been a large number of complaints received by the police. Many middle-aged men of average height report that they've been asked to remove their hats and expose their left ear to prove that they're not Smith. Most are happy to do so, but some feel this is a form of harassment. Back to you, Gordon."

At least the major stations have stopped simply replaying the footage of my arrest, Vicky thought to herself.

"I'm not sure I can think of a story that causes such hatred in the common person," the anchor said to his co-host. "A trinity of hatred really. First you have Silverthorne, the lightning rod of winner-take-all capitalism. Secondly, Silverthorne is working on an IPO, a transaction where fees are fat, institutional investors are the beneficiaries and the common investor is left in the dust. Lastly, the victims here are widows and orphans!"

Vicky could tell right away that Jane and Fiona were sympathetic to her situation at a personal level, and Vicky knew that the quality of the "house arrest" was largely determined by the relationship she would have with them. Earlier, Vicky had asked politely if she could call her mother, pointing out that her mother was an older lady and would be very confused and upset by the news, if she understood it at all.

After the three of them had seen the newscaster's "trinity

of hatred," Jane declared, "You do need to call your mother."

Vicky smiled, happy that reason had prevailed.

"It'll have to be on speakerphone, so we can listen in," Jane added.

"That's fine," Vicky responded.

— · —

Luke grabbed a flyer with the Polish Centre's opening and closing times. He then went the couple of hundred yards to the Tekno Bar he'd spotted on Friday. The inside of the store had that hard, modern brightness of tech, space and chrome. It seemed to have a wide selection of brand-name phones and computer products on the shelves. There were printers and copiers. It was not what he had pictured on Friday when he'd read the sign that included *Barbershop* in the list of services.

From behind the counter, a scruffy-looking twenty-something asked if he could help. Luke pulled his laptop out of his backpack and pointed to where the battery would go in. The kid seemed to understand and pulled a battery off a nearby shelf. Luke held up two fingers. The kid's expression turned to one of doubt and he ducked into the back room. Luke didn't know if that was a good thing or a bad thing. He noticed someone was doing a money transfer. He felt his heart speeding up. He felt the sweat gathering beneath his skin, about to erupt through. Another person stood behind him. Luke could feel himself gulping for air, and tried to control his breathing. He glanced at the door. If he broke and ran, how much of a start would he have. Three seconds? Maybe as many as five? Would that be enough?

For Christ's sake, he wasn't some spy or hardened criminal. He was a desk jockey, a pencil pusher, a pocket-protector nerd. He thought in numbers, bytes and calculations. There was being outside his comfort zone and then there was this. This was crazy. This was nuts. This was just plain stupid.

He went wet with sweat. Apparently, he had a sweat gland beneath every single pore of his skin, and they were now watering heavily. This kid was taking forever. And to do what? What exactly was taking so damn long? Luke looked again at the door. His sweat-soaked clothes seem to clutch tightly onto his body, suffocating him. He felt sick, head swimming with the nausea of an early flu.

That was it, Luke decided, he was out of there. He turned on his heel and made it a step or two before he heard, "Hey!"

His head snapped around.

The kid smiled and waved his arm. In his hands was a similar battery. Luke lumbered back, his eyes darting. The kid explained with considerable detail, relishing the chance to show off his expertise, that it was for an earlier model from a different manufacturer, but that he was very sure it would work. Luke held up a hand for him to stop, gave a thumbs up, paid for both batteries with cash and staggered out.

He walked blindly for a few blocks, just waiting for his heart to slow and the sweat to cool. There was no tidal wave of relief. There was no euphoria. There was instead a near-continuous slowly easing blood-thump in his ears. Technically, that had gone well. But equally, it had been awful. If he didn't figure out the dataset immediately, Luke was going to give himself a heart attack.

Focus on your breathing, he told himself. Breathing regularly and deeply, he went to another charity shop. There, he bought a two-piece set of hard-sided rolling luggage, where the smaller piece fitted inside the larger. He could really use that. And some more clothing. The total came to £48. He put down three twenties, refused the change and the receipt and headed out of the store.

All of this happened without him speaking one word. He was learning to communicate without speaking.

Who would have thought that keeping his mouth shut would

be a survival skill?

— . —

The top floor of the New Scotland Yard building on Victoria Embankment was fully taken up by conference rooms. The small chalkboard outside the largest room read *Smith*. The room's walls were covered by whiteboards, smart-screens, chalkboards and easels with large pads of cheap paper. The table in the middle was covered with laptops and landline phones as well as left-over food-and-drink containers.

The case was similar to the escape of a prisoner. There was a set of protocols to follow. They had pictures, fingerprints and considerable knowledge of the person they sought. It was very convenient that he had such a distinguishing visual characteristic: the disfigured left ear.

Constable Zofia Dabrowski had finally managed to get the attention of her supervisor and his boss. She and another officer had searched Smith's hotel room on Friday morning. Since then, she'd manned the phones. But something about the search of the room kept nagging at her. She had the feeling that the room had been searched before she and her partner had got there. Some of the furniture was slightly askew. The dresser drawers weren't properly shut, even though there was nothing in them. There were no obvious signs of a struggle, but the room just didn't look as presentable as one would expect. The bed was unmade, but Smith hadn't picked up his *Financial Times* newspaper from outside the door that morning.

She felt there was a chance that Smith had been kidnapped by someone who wanted the data.

She'd been debating the pros and cons of coming forward with her theory. It was not recommended that constables in their late twenties have a "hunch" in a high-profile case. On the other hand, they were all trained to think things over and present ideas at the Met, no matter the ranks of the participants.

She fully expected the obvious questions: how did anyone

else know he had the data without inside knowledge of what he intended to do? So it had to be an inside job. And why not just steal the data, which was a whole lot more transportable than the numbers geek, and which this insider clearly understood the value of?

They were also trained not to take blowback personally.

Chief Inspector Sean McConley, Zofia's boss's boss, narrowed his eyes when he grasped Zofia's theory and its implications. As others questioned Zofia, he confessed to himself he hadn't thought of it. He mulled it over. Did stealing data, even something as innocuous as mortality stats, have implications for national security? If it didn't, could he make it have national security implications? *Yes*, he thought, *he probably could.*

A threat to national security meant that they'd have to pull in MI5, the branch that dealt with terrorism and espionage. The Met would never say it aloud, but MI5 had much better cyber theft skills than the Met did. Plus, the political angle. Public awareness of this case was off the charts. If the Met couldn't find Smith, it would be quite the black eye. And the Met didn't need any more of those. He knew the Superintendent would see that angle immediately.

McConley still wanted to be the one to present the theory to his boss, the Superintendent. Even if outlandish, it could be an escape clause. That is, from the perspective of administration, which he was in up to his balls already.

The meeting dispersed and people made their way back to their desks and offices. McConley walked to Zofia's desk and, standing close to her side, said in a hushed tone, "I will set up a call for us with MI5 sometime tomorrow."

— · —

Luke wondered how a charity shop could possibly pay high-street rent by selling things so cheap, even donated things. He had always used logic to understand everything he encountered. This approach to the world had served him well from the start of his career, when he sat his actuarial and computer programming exams, all the way to his later roles in investment banking and risk management.

From time to time, he wondered if he was missing some form of beauty in things that weren't perfectly logical. Since there was nothing he could do about it, he shrugged off that concern – which was a logical response.

Now he had to think differently. He had to think like a fugitive. So far, he was barely scraping a pass. And if he failed, he'd be a dead man.

As he headed to his little park, Furnivall, he approached a homeless woman sitting on the pavement with her back against a low stone wall and her legs outstretched, leaving only a couple of feet of pavement on which to pass. She looked at him pulling the luggage and drew her legs in, giving Luke enough space to roll past. "You're welcome," she said, as though she was some type of toll booth and he was obliged to at least give thanks for his passage. He nodded politely instead.

As he rolled past the curled-up legs of the woman, he knew that he had to steer clear of other homeless people. He'd be a big, easy payday for them, and they had time to devote to collecting the twenty thousand. There could even be service providers for the homeless who might see him in Furnivall and approach him.

As Luke came out of the tunnel to Furnivall Gardens, he ground to a halt. He needed a plan to get back into his camp. There were a couple of narrow paths into the park from the pavement along the motorway. Crashing into the brush with a piece of roller luggage could create a spectacle, and there were people milling about. He waited until the little park was empty.

When the right moment came, he smashed in.

It was a fiasco. One of the wheels got tangled with a vine, and he had to lift the luggage and break the vine to keep moving and get out of sight. The wheel might never work again. A dead branch, stiff and pointed, got him on the right shoulder and another got him on the neck. A passer-by could easily have noticed. And the symbolism sucked.

He was relieved to be back in his room. Dead leaves were his carpet. Green leaves were his walls and ceiling. The discomfort of getting from the path into the brush was actually a good thing. The more impenetrable, the better. It wasn't a room. It was a fortress.

He started the jetboil then pulled out a cardboard cup of quinoa and black beans as he began organising.

He unzipped the large piece of luggage, pulled out the smaller piece and unzipped it as well. He dug shallow holes in the ground so that both would be partly underground, with just enough room to unzip them. Once partly buried, they were much harder to see and easier to cover with branches and leaves, the way he had covered his large backpack that morning. Hopefully rain or dampness would not penetrate through the zips, and the plastic bags inside the luggage would be a backup. The small piece of luggage held the food and the larger one the clothes. He pulled everything out of his large backpack and some of the things out of the small one. As he packed his makeshift wardrobe into the larger suitcase, he thought through everything he had. When he saw the jacket he'd purchased from the beggar back in Hyde Park, his hands stopped and his stomach tied itself into a knot. *Where was the hat?*

Frantically he looked everywhere and couldn't find it.

In his enthusiasm for the turban, he'd probably left the floppy hat in the changing room at the charity store.

There's nothing I can do now, he reasoned. Hopefully it was a popular style and colour so no one would hand it in and say, the guy who bought the black turban left it. Hopefully the charity shop had already put it up for sale with all the other gardening hats, waiting for its new owner.

The cup of quinoa and black beans were delicious and devoured in less than a minute. The empty cardboard cup itself looked tempting.

The next step would be to rebury the large backpack. He had one plastic bag that was big enough for his sleeping bag. When he wasn't using the sleeping bag it would go into the plastic bag and then into the big backpack. He couldn't count on the pack being watertight.

He thought about what he knew so far. It appeared that some of BMI's most recent financial results had been shown as being better than they actually were.

Had BMI deliberately tweaked the results? Any company approaching an IPO would want to show not just higher earnings, but growth in the years immediately before the IPO. A higher rate of growth would increase the amount that investors were willing to pay to be the owners of that earnings stream in the future. If that was what had happened, BMI would certainly do anything in their power to stop Luke from exposing it. Could it be that simple?

BMI's auditors would have caught this. There's a reason why they got paid. It was exactly to stop this kind of book cooking. Besides, he'd calculated the difference between actual claims and claim totals for a total of six consecutive years. The differences swung back and forth between positive and negative. If cooking was taking place, then the chef was lousy.

— . —

Braun was sitting at the table in his office when Drinkwater opened the door. Ten minutes late, dressed like he's on his way to dinner and acting like nothing else mattered, Braun observed silently.

What a tosser, Braun thought.

With a casual nod, Drinkwater sat beside Braun and started reading the legal-sized pad of yellow lined paper that Braun pushed in front of him.

On the first page were outcomes where Smith didn't find anything in the data. The scenario at the top of the page was the one where Smith either turned himself in or was found by the police or a civilian. That was the easy one. The outcome was a press conference which might include a cash reward if a civilian was responsible for finding Smith. Drinkwater read silently.

Much more troubling was a scenario in the middle of the page where Smith simply dumped the raw data onto the internet. Drinkwater put his finger on it. "What would motivate him to do that?" he asked.

"Maybe he tries to crowdsource a solution. If someone else could solve the puzzle, he would at least be partly vindicated."

"This guy's pretty sharp, you think?"

"Very sharp. He's pointed out that we haven't outsourced our policyholder admin and that we don't share any of our mortality risk with reinsurers, which means we are outliers for not having any outside companies under the hood with us. So he's sharp analytically, but he has his antennae up for governance-related stuff as well," Braun pointed out. "He's probably thinking through this same list as we sit here."

"So, all the outcomes under data dumping are very bad for us, aren't they?"

"They certainly are. But they're also bad for him."

— · —

It was inky dark when the lightning bolt struck Luke.

When it finally occurred to him, the answer was so obvious that if another actuary had been involved he'd have been embarrassed.

Insurance accounting included a concept known as IBNR, *Incurred But Not Reported*. When an insurer closes its books to produce financial statements, there will be claims on their policies that have just occurred but have not been reported to them yet. Therefore, an estimation of the value of these claims was included in the financial results. In hindsight, that estimation would have been too high in some years, and too low in others. The variation between the estimate of the late claims and the actual late claims was the variation he was seeing in his analysis. There was nothing nefarious about it at all.

He felt a spasm of genuine anger at himself. He was going to have to be way smarter to get to the bottom of all this.

Eventually, the anger faded as exhaustion took over. His eyelids felt as heavy as lead and closed of their own accord.

— · —

"The next scenario is no garden party," Drinkwater remarked. "He figures it out. Then: extortion."

"If he tries anything public, no matter what it is, we can nail him on the non-disclosure agreement that he and all the bankers signed," said Braun. "Crowdsourcing. Public announcement. Release to a blogger or vlogger or journalist. He can't do anything with the information or we can destroy him; we sue and he ends up in court and eventually in jail. That's the whole point of an NDA. It silences."

"He can still destroy us without going public," Drinkwater observed. "The extortion would have to be private. Clearly the man's a gambler, rolling the dice to see what he can get out of us. He's got the numbers and he's going to use them to make himself richer than Midas. But secretly. This is how I'd do it. I'd threaten to leak it anonymously to Wikileaks. He knows that we can't afford that. We'll have to pay through the nose to keep it private. He'll laugh at us all the way to the bank."

"And we won't be able to touch him."

"That's why I like the last one better."

"The one where Smith is never heard from again?" Braun paused. "Are the resources you've hired still working towards that?

"That's correct."

He may be a tosser but he's a useful tosser. With even more useful connections.

"How would you guarantee that your resources will be successful?"

"I've been given assurances."

The lead of Braun's mechanical pencil suddenly snapped off and rolled across the page. Drinkwater had never seen this happen with Braun, although Braun wrote in pencil all the time. For the first time he really looked at Braun and realised how tense Braun was around that particular outcome.

What a loser, Drinkwater thought. *Getting stressed about this part of the problem. You don't see me snapping any pencils. Mind you, he's good with numbers.*

CHAPTER 3:
Sunday

When Luke woke up, he felt well rested as he breathed the dark air deep into his lungs. The occasional sound of a car had replaced the daytime drone of traffic. Otherwise, it was totally quiet.

He pulled his clothes on and opened his laptop. The keyboard light was all he needed to work on his laptop and would probably not be visible outside the bushes. He was eager to find the answer to the first important question of the day: did the new batteries have power in them?

The answer was yes. Both were almost fully charged. He'd have the power he needed to start the next stage of analysis.

Over recent decades, mortality rates in the developed world had decreased steadily. While this improvement had slowed or even reversed among the population for middle-aged men due to 'deaths of despair', the impact on insurers was muted as fewer of those deaths had been insured.

BMI had been quick to disclose that its mortality results, averaged over ten years, were consistent with the insurance industry. However, there were two reasons that potential investors in the IPO would want to know more.

First and most important, many insurers were accessing new data sources to include in their analysis of an applicant's mortality risk. "Big Data" (the capture of driving records, credit histories, pharmacy records, etc) combined with artificial intelligence could influence an insurer's decisions to insure or not. Or at what price. Insurance industry analysts, who had seen this development through insurtech mergers and capital raisings, were wary of traditional insurers, such as BMI, who were seemingly stuck in the dark ages, dipping their feathered quills in inkpots and signing off their missives with hot wax and a signet ring.

Were these new IT approaches cherry-picking the best risks and thereby leaving insurers such as BMI with a riskier pool of new policyholders? If so, the rate of BMI's mortality improvement would be lower than the industry as a whole. This could be the case even if BMI's mortality results, averaged over a long historical period, had been close to the industry's.

If an analysis over shorter periods of time showed a lower-than-industry rate of improvement, investors would assume this would lead to lower earnings for BMI in the future, and therefore the company would be worth less. For this reason, Luke had requested BMI's data that addressed this concern.

He noticed that the sky had started to lighten. With no people in the park, this would be the best time to explore his surroundings.

He put the laptop into the backpack and pulled it on. He and the laptop would be inseparable until this was solved.

— · —

Smith had dropped his decoys – his phone and his wallet – onto eastbound buses. Since he hadn't gone into the park after the ATM encounter, it would make sense that he'd go west. Today, so would Manny.

He started at the Bureau de Change. If Smith had taken a cab, the cabbie probably would have remembered a passenger wearing a gardener's hat and reported it. Smith had obviously been thinking about buses. If he were Smith, and trying to hide in London, where would he get off the westbound bus?

— · —

Luke hadn't gone far before the park started to fill with people, and he had retreated to his camp. It had been about 48 hours since the shit had hit the fan and he wondered how his patient was doing. His mind drifted back to the first time he encountered the veterans' PTSD camp.

He had taken the wrong line in the Tube, and when he'd looked at the upcoming stops, he'd recognised and chosen Embankment. The walk from there to his hotel wouldn't be too far and would take him past many of London's tourist sights. The sights wouldn't have changed, but he hadn't seen them in a long time.

When he'd stepped out onto the street, he'd stopped and stared across Whitehall Gardens at the Houses of Parliament and Big Ben. He'd seen them hundreds of times, but that was half their beauty. The British Empire had crumbled, but it had played a huge part in world history, and these buildings would always be a majestic testament to that.

Walking through Trafalgar Square towards St James's Park, it would have been hard not to feel that one was in the very heart of Britishness, if there were such a word. Far in the back of his mind, the orchestra started playing *Land of Hope and Glory*. Its deliberate stately tempo made it impossible to stop the music once it started. A graduation procession song in the US where it's referred to as *Pomp and Circumstance*, it's practically a national anthem to the Brits. He remembered an occasion when, at the end of some function at his oldest child's British school, the song played and parents all spontaneously began to sing. He was told that the King enjoyed this song so much when it was first played in the very early 1900s that he demanded lyrics be written. Luke associated the song with British patriotism.

Proceeding down The Mall, he'd had no need to deal with all the tourists around Buckingham Palace, and veered towards

Hyde Park. When he'd seen the camp, he'd stopped and chatted with one of the veterans, getting the quick history and purpose. If Buckingham Palace was most certainly the "Glory" in *Land of Hope and the Glory*, then these guys must represent "Hope", he remembered thinking as he stuffed a couple of twenties into the jar.

— . —

On his third ride west on the bus, Manny got off at Ravenscourt Park. It was the one place where some tree cover would have been visible from the bus. That would probably have been attractive to Smith's eye.

He was surprised by the amount of activity in Ravenscourt Park. Granted, it was a sunny Sunday, but there were kids playing basketball, the football pitch was packed and the tennis courts were full. The pool was absolutely teeming with children and attentive parents. It was a busy place, but there were decent-sized sections with trees and bushes. For someone trying to hide, this seemed like a possibility.

— . —

"We're in the money, lads!" one of the men said softly. On the hillside at Ravenscourt Park were some dense bushes with a man sitting on a bench. He fitted Smith's general description and wore very large headphones. The men glanced at each other.

"Jocko, you go do the honours," one man suggested. "The rest of us will stay here."

"Yes sir," Jocko said with some surprise.

He walked quickly to the bench and as he approached, noticed that the man had a particularly intense odour. He sat down on the bench to the man's left. The man looked over and looked up and down at Jocko's fatigues and high black boots. He was visibly nervous. "Morning," Jocko said, without making eye contact. "Nice headphones," he added after a pause. The homeless man turned towards him, pulled the earphone away from his right ear – the one farthest from Jocko – and said:

"Sorry, I missed that."

"Just saying hello and complimenting your earphones."

"They're great. I have a receipt for 'em."

"I'd like to buy some too. Do you mind if I look at them?"

The man put the right earphone back in place and stared straight ahead, not saying a word but looking even more nervous than before.

Jocko walked back to the group. He told them about the very suspicious behaviour of removing the right-ear covering when the left would have made more sense. The man looked and smelled like he had been homeless for some time but had a few days' growth on his chin which would have been about right for Smith. He was also wearing large sunglasses. He didn't seem to have an American accent, but the conversation had been short.

A local resident walking her dog in the park noticed the group of a dozen or so men in army fatigues. They were hard to miss. When she saw them watching a homeless man, she stopped immediately and texted the police. Two policemen arrived in minutes, just as the veterans were walking up to the man on the bench. "Gentlemen, gentlemen, what's going on here?" one of the policemen asked.

Jocko started to answer at the same time as the homeless man. The policeman held up his hand in Jocko's direction. "I'd like to hear from the other gentleman first," he said.

"These men wanted to look at my headphones and I said no. Then they surrounded me."

"Sir, can you please take off the headphones? It's important you hear the whole conversation clearly," the policeman said.

The homeless man took off the headphones.

The policeman turned to Jocko. "And you were saying?"

"Officer, this proud group of veterans is based in Green Park. We help the City of London with the sanitation of Hyde Park, Green Park and St James's Park. Today we are doing the same here." Jocko pointed to a couple of bin liners strapped to team members. "As an additional public service, we are on the lookout for that criminal-at-large Luke Smith. As everyone knows, his left ear is disfigured. This gentleman looked suspicious to us, and we politely requested him to remove his headphones in order to confirm whether this gentleman was Smith or not."

As the last words were leaving Jocko's mouth, the policeman started talking over him. "You can see clearly now he's not Smith. Everyone appreciates your service to the nation and to the city. Going forward, however, please use the hotline to inform us of any information regarding Smith, and leave the actual policing to us. Cheerio, then," the policeman said, signalling the end of the conversation.

As the discussion progressed, a small crowd had begun to form around the veterans. A few people were taking pictures with their phones or recording the conversation.

Manny Chapman happened to see the incident developing from a distance. He wasn't close enough to hear the discussion, but he had a pretty good idea what was happening. And it gave him an idea.

— . —

Jane was helping Vicky make her bed. Vicky had offered Jane and Fiona the opportunity to bring their laundry with them to her flat. Folding clothes had become a group activity, and making the bed was the natural conclusion of the laundry task.

Vicky could see Jane's eyes fixed on the rose on her nightstand, which had sagged considerably and would soon become mouldy.

"Okay, the rose needs to go. But first we need to hear the story."

Vicky picked up the miniature vase carefully and brought it to the kitchen. She looked away as she dumped it into the kitchen rubbish. She didn't want that to be her last memory of the rose.

"Fiona, come quick, this has potential," Jane said loudly enough that Fiona could hear from the other room.

"Hmm, where to start," Vicky began, standing by the window and looking out. She had never spoken about her feelings for Luke.

"It was Thursday and the team had gone out for drinks. When I arrived, there were already many empty pitchers of beer. There's some kind of statue or sculpture in this beer garden, people in a boat. It's pretty much life-sized. One of the genius lawyers on the team decided we should all get in the boat for a team picture, saying something about us rowing together, like Argonauts."

Vicky paused to raise her eyebrows at the knuckleheaded ideas that her male colleagues all thought were brilliant. Jane and Fiona grinned back.

"They all started to pile in. I made it clear that I'd take the picture. For heaven's sake, I'm in a skirt with heels. Just as I finally had everyone spaced, a passer-by offered to take the picture. Of course. So I had to be in it. It was impossible to disagree.

"Luke was at the back of the boat and helped me up. Our faces came very close in the process. I was behind him and there was no room for me to move to the front. As I pushed his shoulders down to lower him a bit so that my face would be visible, I realised that everyone was in front of us and looking straight ahead. I pushed my chest into his back as hard as I could. I did it long enough to make sure that he knew it wasn't a mistake, that I hadn't just lost my balance or something."

Jane and Fiona both took an audible breath. Fiona overdramatically fanned her face with her hand.

"I couldn't believe I did it. I've never done anything that even borders on that. He's working for me on this project."

"I believe that's illegal," said Fiona to Jane, who "tsked tsked" with a grin.

"Then two policemen walked up. Seeing them, the group all tried to talk at once. A boatload of drunken alphas acting like schoolboys." There was a round of headshakes from the three women.

"Your Met brethren dutifully informed us that it's not legal to climb on a statue or to drink alcohol while you are climbing on a statue. But they added that it wouldn't be a problem as long as we were to cease and desist immediately. Seconds later we were all awkwardly trying to exit the boat. All at the same time.

"Within a few minutes it was just Luke and me left in the beer garden while I paid the bill. It felt a little awkward because I could tell that we both wanted to be with each other but there wasn't much we could do about it before this bloody deal was done.

"Now I'm just so grateful that the police hadn't taken our group picture. Nothing personal ladies, but I would hate to think of all of our high-finance mug shots, illegally on a statue, being downloaded into some Met database."

"Wait, where does the rose come into this?" Jane asked eagerly.

"We walked through that big pedestrian shopping centre. It was easy to tell he was nervous and trying hard to find something to talk about. He pointed out the bike shop where he had bought a jersey when he was in London with his sons on holiday a couple of years ago. Apparently, he likes to bike. It seems he's pretty athletic."

Jane cut in. "Is that based on groping or visuals?" They giggled.

"Both, I guess. We were kind of going towards Liverpool Street Station, but not directly and not quickly. We got into the narrow streets, and I thought about pushing him into one of those little alleyways in the hopes of... I don't know, maybe some kissing and groping. At one point, the backs of our hands brushed together, and we both looked sideways at each other. I'm sure he was thinking exactly what I was thinking ... wouldn't it be nice to be holding hands right now."

Jane and Fiona sighed in unison.

"I had a car service waiting for me, so I told him I would walk him to the Tube. Just inside the station, there was a newsagent shop and we turned in so I could pick up a paper for the ride home. He sees one of those single roses that you sometimes see for sale in those places, buys it and stands directly in front of me, holding it in two hands. He says how much he is enjoying the assignment, and how lucky he was that I'd tracked him down. He said that at the same time he was anxious for the deal to be finished, to see what would happen immediately after. And then he hands me the rose." She drew a shaky breath and wiped her eye.

"Honest to God, I think my heart did flutter. A spontaneous act of affection. When did that last happen to me?"

"Sounds like you wish you'd ridden the Tube with him all the way back to his hotel."

"And then maybe ridden ..." Fiona stopped talking and pulled her hand up to her mouth quickly as Jane playfully slapped her shoulder and Vicky laughed.

Vicky couldn't help but think that if only she had slept with Luke, she probably wouldn't have lost track of him the next morning. Then she wouldn't be living with a GPS bracelet on her ankle and the police at her kitchen table.

— · —

The third battery was running out of power. At least Luke had judged that one correctly. His own energy level was also at its minimum. In his new ecosystem, the two seemed to be linked.

He had the results now, but he'd seen what was coming hours ago.

Ten years ago, BMI's results were good by industry standards. They had gradually worsened over the following five years and then they had turned a corner and improved. In the last couple of years they had suddenly become much, much better. The recent success was something BMI should have been trumpeting. But they weren't.

Again, he was baffled.

As it was getting dark quickly, Luke crawled into his sleeping bag. Looking straight up, about half of his view was the leaves of the trees and the other half was the sky. There were a few cirrus clouds high in the sky, looking like tufts of hair, floating very slowly to the east. The last light of the sun was hitting the clouds in such a way that there was a pink tinge to them. He wondered how many people, in how many different sets of circumstances, might be admiring the same clouds. He thought about eyes looking up and he pictured Vicky's blue eyes getting wider as she looked up at him with the rose in her hand.

CHAPTER 4:
Monday

Amber paused at the door to her boss's office. Her boss had just arrived for the day and the door was still ajar, so Amber was confident she was not interrupting any deep thinking. She put on her most professional but open smile and knocked lightly.

"Hey, can I pick your brain for a minute?"

"Of course, but if it takes more than two minutes then I will have to bill you," her boss responded with a smile.

"I spent some of my spare time since Friday analysing what I could with the BMI data we had, and I think I've found something."

Her boss's expression immediately hardened. She moved quickly past Amber to shut the door to her office.

"The trend of the mortality within the last ten years –"

Her boss spoke over her. "Compliance has told us in no uncertain terms that everything to do with that BMI assignment is out of bounds. You are back here now full time. There is no BMI assignment or team."

"But I thought maybe if …"

"No ifs here," her boss cut her off again sternly. "When it comes to compliance, you either have a clean record or you don't. You've put me in a very awkward position just with this off-the-record conversation."

Her boss turned away from her, walked back behind her desk and sat down, her face like thunder. "I will do you an enormous favour and not report you. But if this happens again, you can be guaranteed it will go on your compliance record. I won't have anyone work with me who does not have a clean record." There was a heartbeat of silence then her boss snapped, "Understood?"

It was not a question. Amber nodded anyway and mumbled, "I'm so sorry." Then she slunk out of the office and along the hall towards the ladies' room.

It was too early in the morning for anyone to be in the loo. Amber stood in front of the mirror, her eyes focused on something other than her own reflection. Then she threw herself away and stalked to a stall and locked herself in. There she stood. Not pacing within the cubicle or even jiggling. She just stood, preternaturally still. She felt like kicking and punching the shit out of the walls. Instead, she let the chaos of emotion sweep over her and through her and around her. Like grit in a tumbling stream, she let it all foam and churn and kick up inside her.

If she screwed up on this, could she somehow lose her status in the UK? Her parents, who had moved from Hong Kong back to the village in China to care for their own parents, were depending on her. They were depending on her not just for money, but for hope.

The minutes passed. Amber let them. She'd been here before. She knew how to handle this. She put no effort into anything. She just waited.

If she lost her job or was unable to leverage this job into something more lucrative, what would her parents and grandparents live on? What would she live on? The idea terrified her. But her rage at being smacked down like a two-year-old having a tantrum was pretty powerful too.

Bit by bit the whirl inside her slowed. She let the clarity rise as the grains of red-hot grit settled. And with the real calmness came insight.

She hated herself. Not for thinking her boss would be receptive, that'd been just plain foolish. What'd she think her boss was going to say: *Break the rules. I don't care. What the hell, let me help.*

Dumb. Silly. Stupid. She was here for a reason: to support the family. So she had to play the game by its rules. And that meant she had to keep her head down and do as she was told and work hard and suck it up with a smile on her face.

She knew that. She'd known that for a long time. It had been drilled into her. She knew the price of failure. This spasm of silliness would not happen again. Not ever.

And still she stood there. Her rage went deeper than that.

She'd hated herself for a long time. She'd hated the choices she'd made in life, her own goals and ambitions – what she'd given up in order to get where she was.

Back in 2020 in Hong Kong, she hadn't joined her friends at the protests.

Ever since, she hadn't liked what she saw in the mirror.

— . —

Manny and Simon set off in Simon's taxi to Buckingham Palace. As if they were tourists. Simon was five years younger than Manny and it was clear early on that he would always be in his older brother's shadow, not living up to the same status in school and sports. He'd felt Manny's cold disdain whenever he had to wade into a fight to bail his younger brother out. And he'd suffered more than his fair share of bruises as Manny would punch him, casually but forcefully, just because.

He'd been in year six and Manny had been doing his GCSEs at a posh boarding school when their father had been killed in action. Simon went to the local comprehensive, which he rather liked. People there were really very nice. But he decided not to follow Manny into the military. Instead, he sat in an uncle's spare room while he went through the laborious task of acquiring the "knowledge" of roads and traffic one needed to pass the test to be a London cabbie.

Driving suited Simon. He enjoyed the fleeting moments of interaction with passengers and with other cabbies. He always refused to join other cabbies at the pub, as drinking was a waste of money. They had an arrangement that worked very well when Manny was on one of his "assignments." Simon and his taxi provided secure, anonymous transportation. There were few streets in London where a taxi couldn't just wait with its availability light on the roof turned off. It never caught anyone's attention or looked suspicious. Manny paid him extremely well for this, which meant his family was a little better padded, his children a little better provided for. He didn't know how Manny got started doing what he did. He didn't need to know and didn't particularly want to know. Simon liked to keep things simple.

Manny found the Green Beret's camp easily when he entered Green Park. He stopped to read the sign explaining the plight of the veterans and how assistance to these veterans was insufficient to non-existent. He was hoping that by walking close to the camp he would spot Jocko, rather than having to ask for him. Lurking was one of his skills, and eventually he spotted Jocko. As Manny walked towards him, Jocko noticed him before he entered the camp area. He shook Jocko's hand and patted him on the right shoulder at the same time. Manny motioned that they should walk together away from the camp.

"How's your search for that cabbage-eared cunt going?"

"Not so well. We've been through the parks here and Ravenscourt. We've found a few vagrants in the park with cabbage for brains who thought they were Smith and kept trying to turn themselves in." The two men snorted in half-disgust half-amusement. "But that's all we found," Jocko finished dejectedly.

"Too bad," Manny responded. "I thought some more about our conversation yesterday and would like to bring you into a better plan to find the cunt. This is something between you and me, you can't say anything about this to your buddies here. There are folks who will pay more than twenty grand to find this guy and to make sure that data he has never sees the light of day. Help me find him and you'll get a bigger share of a bigger pot than you will here," Manny said motioning with his head towards the camp.

Manny extended the phone to Jocko, who looked very confused. "If you and your gang get close to him, call me with this phone."

"I don't have training on this equipment, Sergeant." Jocko held the phone like it was a royal child he didn't trust himself to hold.

"It's easy," Manny said. He showed Jocko how to turn it on, and how to make an outgoing call to his number, the only number that was in the contacts.

"Don't let your buddies see the phone, and never ever give out my number," Manny added.

"Won't I need to charge it?"

"No, just don't turn it on unless you need to call me. The battery will last if you leave it off. Won't take us long to find this piece of shit."

Jocko couldn't take his eyes off the phone.

"I look forward to working together again," Manny said, extending a small bottle of Scotch towards Jocko.

"Thanks Sergeant. I'm looking forward to it as well," Jocko said, looking down at the bottle. "I'm afraid I can't accept this gift though … no booze allowed in the camp."

"That's good discipline on your part Smith, and poor discipline on mine," Manny responded after a moment's thought.

— · —

Dieter Braun had joined BMI in his late twenties and was about to celebrate his twentieth anniversary there, though now was not the time for celebration. His experience at one of the

German mutual insurance companies was all it took to get his foot in the door at BMI. He had stepped past – and some might say on – many people in the finance department to quickly attain the department's highest level. To the best of his staff's knowledge, he had no friends, only colleagues. He had no outside interests, only appropriate charities. He didn't chat at the café while picking up a coffee or attend the Friday night drinks.

The best single word to describe Dieter Braun would be precise. Somehow, his perfectly shaped bald head, the sharpness of his nose and chin, his tailored suits, all conveyed precision. He was always so cleanly shaven that it seemed as if he'd just come from a hot-towel straight-razor barber. The edges of his rimless glasses looked like they could cut skin. He was never late for a meeting.

And controlling. Precise and controlling. Braun owned the master finance spreadsheet and no number left his department that he didn't double-check himself.

That day, he had made a concerted attempt to present himself as "business as usual". Yet he'd cancelled many of his previously scheduled meetings, locked the door to his office a couple of times and gone through all the scenarios that Drinkwater had outlined several times.

Years ago, Braun had devised a scheme, an outrageous stunt that would earn tens of millions. Millions upon millions. Tax free. Invisible. Free money.

The previous CEO had been a full partner in it. After he passed away three years ago, Braun had debated whether he should disclose it to the new CEO, Alaistair Drinkwater, or shut it down. Braun had watched as Drinkwater went through money at a rate that would take even the wealthiest by surprise, and guessed that the new CEO could use the extra cash.

To take a company public, it was extremely useful to have a charming and good-looking front man, and Drinkwater had a genetic endowment of an ear-to-ear smile, chiselled jaw and thick luxurious hair. He was a man who knew everyone who counted, who showed up at every important fundraiser and then worked the room as if he was aiming to be the prime minister but chose not to engage with that level of silliness and instead chose business. The walking talking personification of British Mutual Insurance was Alaistair Drinkwater. His only downside was his avarice.

An IPO would make Alaistair Drinkwater rich beyond even his wildest dreams.

The one thing that Braun knew was greed. And what it did to people.

Braun decided that Drinkwater would not examine anything too closely. But Drinkwater should know something in case he was needed to smooth uncertainties or had to redirect attention elsewhere or sideline a questioner. In case Braun needed someone to do something dirty. So Drinkwater needed to know enough but not too much.

The only remaining trace of the scheme was deep in administrative files. They had debated the pros and cons of "cleansing" the file. There would be too big a risk, Braun had argued. Any time you went back and changed a data file, you risked someone internal – or even an auditor – noticing. Best to let sleeping dogs lie.

When that risk passed, Braun was able to sleep at night. Disclosing it later would have left Drinkwater open to the legitimate criticism that he hadn't disclosed it as soon as he'd learned about it. It made Drinkwater complicit.

They were an odd couple, but this had somehow made them inseparable bedfellows.

— . —

Zofia checked her watch as she walked into the helter-skelter of the large conference room. Hopefully her late arrival would go unnoticed in the chaos.

"Oh, there you are. Let's go talk to our friends over at MI5." Chief Inspector McConley's voice floated over her shoulder. Guess she'd been noticed.

She hustled to catch up with McConley as he left the large room. She was surprised when he headed to the elevator. Zofia expected they'd use one of the smaller empty rooms on that floor for a conference call. When the elevator got to the ground floor and they left the New Scotland Yard building, she realised they were physically going to the MI5 building.

As they walked, he asked how long she had been in the force, and where she had grown up. She described how she'd come to the UK from Poland as a student, met and married a Polish contractor in London and never even considered going back to Poland. She told him how she'd joined the force in the technology group. It had taken a couple of years, until all the excitement had been ground up and baked into her day-in day-out, that she realised she was far more interested in what was done with data than in actually producing it.

"I remember when I was new to the force, I kept my mouth shut for years. Finally, I spoke up on a case. I can still picture how high my commander was able to raise his eyebrows. I thought there was an angle to the case that no one else seemed to have seen."

He stopped and looked straight into her brown eyes. Her hair was dark blonde and shoulder length. They both realised that they were the exact same height.

"In the end, my idea was complete bollocks," he said, shrugging ruefully. "But from that point on I had the confidence to blurt out just about any idea I had. Soon after that, my commander started to ask my opinion. Others saw that and started to ask me what I thought."

They started walking again, their conversation returning to the Smith case.

"We'll meet with Chief Inspector Ross, whom I've known

for some time," McConley said. "Once you've outlined your theory, he and I will want to carry on with a bunch of procedural stuff."

"Yes, of course. I will make sure I don't overstay."

So, there are *leaders with people skills in the Met after all,* she thought to herself. Her direct boss was completely focused on the hours and minutes that everyone worked, petty details in reports and other minutiae. He kept pronouncing her name with an *S* and not a *Z* and used sports analogies she didn't understand for everything.

She wanted so badly to make an impression on McConley before she left on maternity leave. The Smith case was the perfect opportunity.

— · —

"Welcome to Medjool Market," the man behind the register said in a leathery voice, surprising Luke. He nodded in return in the affirmative and made a greater degree of eye contact than he had made with anyone in the last few days.

As Luke walked the half block to the Polish Centre, he realised that the man in the store recognised him as a regular customer. That was a good sign. He was starting to blend in.

Or maybe not. He was no longer a faceless forgettable unknown, just another quiet brown-skinned Sikh. Now he was recognised. Which meant he was recognisable.

In the final few steps to the door of the Polish Centre, Luke noticed a homeless man standing with a jar outreached. He froze for a split second as the man made eye contact with him. It was the crazy homeless guy from Ravenscourt Park. Luke pulled his gaze away, entered the building and stopped to process what had just happened. At the moment, the homeless guy didn't have the aura of craziness about him, but the prominent brow and shoulders, scruffy chin, matted hair and the smell remained the same. He looked like the wax caveman figure you would see in a natural history museum. Luke had gone to school with a similar-looking guy. His nickname had become "Link," short for "Missing Link." Luke realised he had been wearing the floppy hat when he had come into contact with this homeless version of Link back in Ravenscourt. Could this Link draw the link?

Now was not the time to worry about that.

Luke was relieved to see that the library was open, and no librarian worked on weekdays. He noticed a sign that said there was no eating in the library. He hadn't noticed that on Saturday. He put his backpack up on the desktop computer table, pulled out his laptop and plugged it in. He checked to see that the charging icon was lit up and told himself to swap the new batteries in during the day so he would have three batteries worth of laptop power when he left. If, of course, he didn't have it solved by then. Which he fully intended to do.

Luke first needed to break the data into five-year age groups, and then between genders. The choice of five years was an industry standard, because it generally resulted in a "credible" number of lives in each cell. Years ago, Luke explained this to his kids in terms of a dice in one of their card games. If the dice was "fair," you would expect one sixth of your rolls to a be a number six. If it was genuinely random you could roll the dice six times and not get any sixes at all. That wasn't grounds to conclude the dice wasn't fair. Sometimes that's just the way the cookie crumbled. That reality changes if you increase the number of times that you roll the dice. If you rolled them 600 times, you'd expect to roll sixes about 100 times. If you got 200 sixes instead, you could be confident the dice was loaded.

He decided he'd start with the youngest female age group cells first.

— · —

"Whole wheat," Luke said slowly and carefully, the first words he had spoken in days. Mostly he just pointed. But the man in the white apron and hairnet in the cafeteria at the Polish Centre had himself pointed to several loaves of near identical bread and had spoken in Polish.

Luke nodded for a sliced tomato, a bit of lettuce but refused the slice of red onion. He pointed to a dessert and grabbed a bottle of green tea out of the cooler. He paid quickly in cash and put the change in a tip jar. It seemed like the man and woman were in a contest to see who could be the most eager to help, before the tip even landed in the jar.

His sandwich was indeed tuna salad, and perhaps the best he had ever tasted. Perhaps it was some Polish way of flavouring the tuna, or the fact that it was anything other than rice or lentils that made it taste so good. He ate it more quickly than he would have otherwise. The dessert had a small piece of wax paper wrapped most of the way around it. He wanted to save it as some type of reward for that afternoon, but he couldn't stuff it in his backpack or carry it the way it was into the library. There was only one solution. Creamy and fruity and cakey. It was the single most delicious thing he'd eaten for as long as he could remember, although he had no idea what it was.

A picture of Drinkwater and Braun was on the front page of a newspaper a man was holding up to read. It looked like Braun was staring directly at Luke. He shuddered. But once the man abandoned his paper, Luke was on it like a bug on a sweaty neck.

Ironically, Luke's "theft" had drawn a lot of interest in the IPO, and the journalist was clearly showing off, describing the transaction itself:

> In a normal IPO, shares in a company are awarded to the founders who have contributed time and capital to building the company. Shares are also sold to investors, which raises capital for the company.
>
> In a mutual insurance company, a small portion of

policyholder's premiums build up over time to form the company's capital, making the policyholders the owners of the company.

There are no traded shares and therefore no opportunity for an investor to buy up enough shares to exert control over company management.

As a result, it is difficult for mutual companies to raise blocks of capital for acquisitions or large expenditures. Instead, capital builds up glacially over time.

In an IPO of a mutual insurance company, referred to as a demutualisation, policyholders are awarded shares in the company that they can then hold or sell.

Braun's intense stare in the picture was about the only look that Luke had ever seen from him. He remembered describing to members of the IPO that Braun was "aggressively bald." He explained that Braun had a decent density of hair follicles close to the top of his head, probably more than Luke had. But Braun had shaved his entire head where most men would have gone with wispy hair on top and average density hair on the side. Braun's baldness was no doubt a statement that he saw hair as an unnecessary distraction, reinforcing his aura of precision and control. This thing that others spent so much time and anxiety on, he simply had no use for. It had achieved a good laugh out of a group that was serious by nature. Luke wished he could just go back to the rare moment of levity.

One of the other articles Luke had pulled up had his own picture in it. It was probably taken before the start of the IPO assignment. He looked relaxed. And no wonder. Over the decades of work, he'd kept an eye on the maths of when he could retire, and he'd carefully eased himself out of work.

But life has a way of overturning the apple cart. Some very high and unexpected medical expenses within his family, combined with the arrival of babies, not all of them planned, had made him regret his decision. He'd fussed, helpless and un-helpful. Then came Vicky's call with the lucrative opportunity to be part of the IPO team and the chance for subsequent con-sulting opportunities. It had seemed like a godsend.

In hindsight, being content with a more modest retire-ment and letting family members fend for themselves might have been a better choice. Because he certainly wasn't able to help them now.

When he got back up to the library, he went directly into the washroom. He pulled the plastic bag with the shirt, undies and socks out of his backpack. He washed them in the sink, using hand soap from a dispenser and warm water. He wrung them out as well as he could and stuffed them back in the plas-tic bag and into the backpack.

He looked in the mirror. His face was as tanned now as it ever was, and the few days' worth of growth on his chin was dark, with a bit of grey just becoming discernible.

He thought about his lunch. As satisfying as the meal was, he had violated one of his principles: minimising the number of people he was exposed to. Going forward, he would cook one of the rice and lentil bowls in the morning and put it in his backpack for lunch. He would eat it here, in the toilet. Before exiting, he grabbed one of the two extra rolls of toilet paper that were on top of the toilet, as he had on Saturday.

— · —

"Well, hello there, I hope you are calling me to tell me your mornings are getting better," Maria said before Zofia could speak a word. Maria had been Zofia's boss when she first start-ed in the Met's Information Technology department. She had become a mentor and close friend as Zofia had moved up. She was the only person at the Met who Zofia had told about her pregnancy.

"I'm still having my morning talk on the big white phone,

but I think the conversations are getting a little shorter. I got a few winks in last night."

"Shouldn't you be home knitting or painting a room or looking at lists of names or something?"

"Nope, need a favour."

"I live for this stuff," Maria eagerly responded.

"Between you and me, I'm on the Smith case." Zofia paused to let that sink in.

"The mortality thief?" Maria responded in an astonished tone. "Holy shit, girl."

"Chief Inspector McConley and I were over at MI5 earlier today," Zofia added. She paused again and there was silence in return. That was a first.

"Sorry, that was the sound of my jaw hitting the floor. Wow!"

"Anyway, I don't think Smith is as evil as he is made out to be. In fact, I've got a hunch he's been kidnapped for the data." More silence from Maria. Zofia pictured her eyes as wide as they could possibly be. "Can you take the recordings of all the calls that came in on Friday and search for the word *kidnap*? You probably won't get anything other than people who were kidnapped by aliens. Use that data-science AI thing they gave you that'll find related words or sets of words," she instructed Maria.

"Will do, Detective. I'll have to run that tonight, otherwise the lights will dim during the day here, and people will want to know what's going on."

"I owe you lunch."

"Sister, if this works, you're going to name your daughter after me. I'll set it up now and launch it once the daily grind ends."

Zofia smiled as she hung up. She sat down in front of her laptop and typed in, "What is a demutualisation?"

— · —

Luke completed the maths for the female age groups and compared the results across the years.

The pattern that emerged was what one would have expected when looking at any insurance company's female mortality results. Female rates were lower than male rates and had been improving at a slower pace than male rates. There was some variation in that trend from year to year, but nothing more than what would be expected given the number of lives involved. There was no story in the female mortality. No 'aha'. Zip. Zero. Nada. Nothing.

"Fuck," he muttered to himself. Then winced. What if someone had heard him?

He leaned back in the chair and glanced casually around. There was no one there, no one to hear him swearing at an Excel spreadsheet.

His head hung as he closed his eyes. He had made no progress towards the goal that day. Another day over. Another night of camping, semi-fed, a little damp, fearful and confused.

Then he snapped out of it. He packed up his laptop. He had battery power to start doing the maths on males back at his camp.

— · —

Braun moved quickly out of the elevator towards the corner office. He slowed a bit when he felt the eyes of the entire IT Department move directly to him. He was happy to see that the head of Information Technology was in his office. *How could he have let this slip almost an entire business day,* he asked himself.

The IT manager's eyes widened as he saw Braun approaching. The person who was in the office looking directly at the manager saw the look, turned and saw Braun and left the office as though his pants had caught fire.

"Hey," Braun began, closing the door to the office loudly.

"With all this stupid publicity that started on Friday, we can't have our own people talking publicly about it, so we need to get some NDAs in place." He put the document down on the desk and held out a pen.

The manager absorbed this quickly. "So, everyone in management is signing these?" he responded, and then wondered why he had said it that way.

"Yes," Braun lied.

While the manager flipped to the pages that needed to be signed and scribbled, Braun said, "I also need to find …" He held up a note and read "Phillipe." He paused as he considered how to pronounce the surname.

"You missed Phillipe by less than a minute. He leaves early on Mondays to pick his kid up from school."

By the look on Braun's face, the manager realised this was a situation he was expected to help Braun solve. He motioned his head towards the door to the office as he completed the last signature. Braun followed him closely as he moved quickly to an empty cubicle. He picked up a framed picture from the desk of a man, a woman and a ten-year-old boy.

"This is Phillipe. He's wearing a blue-collared shirt today and has a black backpack. He's a small guy, about five foot six, and catches the Northern Line at Moorgate Station to get home."

Braun hit the street running, framed picture in one hand, NDA and pen in the other, weaving between commuters and scanning both pavements for Phillipe.

It seemed hopeless, but Braun carried on, breathing hard and sweating, never more thankful for his height. The one shred of evidence, the email indicating changes to the data file, was in a laptop somewhere on this street.

A shred of reason penetrated his desperation. His picture had been everywhere since Friday and here he was, appearing to run away. How long until that video went viral?

Would he take that risk to mitigate the email risk? Yes, he would.

Just as the station came into view, he saw the hairline, the blue shirt collar, the backpack he was looking for. He dropped a hand on the man's shoulder and panted, "Phillipe?" Phillipe jumped. "Dieter Braun, CFO."

"Yes, yes, I know who you are," Phillipe managed to choke out, his eyes as wide as saucers.

As pedestrians brushed past, Braun said, "Let's duck into that pub just ahead, shall we? I have something urgent to go over with you."

In the booth, Braun put the document in front of Phillipe and arranged the pen beside it. "With all the silliness that started on Friday, legal says we need certain people to sign these."

Phillipe's eyes went down to the document. "This is a non-disclosure agreement. Everyone knows what these are, courtesy of the Post Office scandal."

The word "scandal", spoken loudly in a public place, plucked Braun like he was a violin and he felt himself vibrate. Nonetheless, he remained calm as Phillipe continued to read the document. Braun put his hands under his thighs to stop himself from strangling the nerd.

Braun knew the moment that Phillipe's eyes reached the £50,000 figure. He raised them slowly to meet Braun's. Braun turned crimson red. There was a moment of silence which Braun broke.

"Let me put it to you succinctly, Phillipe." Braun pronounced each word slowly. "I just fired you. You don't work for BMI anymore. You don't have access to anything, and you can't get in the building." He laid a finger on the framed picture of Phillipe and his family and gently pushed it across the table to him. "You can sign this document and instead of £50,000, I'll make it £100,000. Or you can choose not to."

The staring contest continued.

Braun reached for the document, his shoulders turning.

"I'll sign," Phillipe blurted.

— · —

The doors of McMasters pub, at the corner of King and Cromwell, were wide open as Luke walked past. The smell of beer found his nose, seductive as a Paris perfume. What would be better than popping in for some restorative recreation after a workday that hadn't gone well?

Today, the smell of beer and the sound of people enjoying themselves just made him more frustrated.

The homeless lady with her legs across the pavement was at the far end of Cromwell today, close to the road's end and the bushes. He expected they would have the same exchange as they had on Saturday. Instead, she looked up at him, nodded her head in greeting and said, "Hullo. How are ya? I'm Colleen," and then tapped her palm on the pavement next to her.

He went to sit on the pavement against the wall next to her, thought about taking his backpack off and then chose to simply sit on the top of the curb, facing her.

"I had a really discouraging day." And then he caught himself. What was he doing? For all of his reasons for avoiding people, and homeless people in particular, he had just plopped himself down there and then spoken more words aloud than he had in the last three days.

"How about you?" he asked.

"The same. Got fed, that was good. Think I'm better. Gettin' healed." They let her response hang. Oddly enough, he found himself looking intently at her, willing her to speak more. Willing to wait out the pauses. Not even caring that there are pauses because they didn't feel like pauses; they felt like ... life.

"It's so nice to chat," she said, looking straight at him. "Loneliness is what'll kill me," she added, her eyes losing their focus. He let that one hang too.

After a long silence, he couldn't stop himself. "What brings you here?"

Her eyes refocused and she turned back towards him. "I struggled. I struggled as a girl, as a teenager. I always struggled. My only friends were the ones struggling." She let her head fall forward and ran her fingers through brittle, silvery hair.

"But I was making it. Even had a boyfriend once. We had a dog, Winston, my ma and me. Then one day Winston died. In the middle of the green. My ma was so upset that she went to the doctor. He said we should get another dog. That's what killed my ma, the death of the dog."

So her mother was also not entirely stable. It seemed Colleen came by it honestly.

"That was my first manic episode." She kept going, her eyes focused on Luke. "After that I couldn't stop 'em. One after 'nother. Called it Acute Stress Disorder. The doctor said I couldn't care for myself, and I should go to the hospital. The hospital kept me for three days, but they didn't have a bed for me. So, they sent me all the way from Cornwall to a private hospital here in London. Said they had beds there for me. Big fancy bus ride. And they had the bed. Best bed I ever laid in. Said I was outsourced." Another pause.

"I was getting better. I wasn't having the episodes. Least not so bad. But I had no one to talk with. My friends and family were so far away. Not like they have cars or money or anything. Not like we've got a bunch'a fancy phones. The loneliness was crushing me."

Luke found himself sympathising. An unfortunate set of occurrences had put her here on the pavement. Not laziness or bad choices.

"So I discharged myself. Had to get home. I got a meal here. Getting the next meal is the biggest thing so I'm still here. I'll get back to Cornwall soon. I get some work at some of the charity shops here. Sortin' and foldin'. I can even use the cash register. It's just a few quid now and then."

Even after just a couple of days of solitude, he craved personal interaction of any sort. The frustration he felt minutes ago was gone, replaced by the thought: *There but for the grace of God, go I*. Colleen refocused on Luke.

"Yourself?"

Although it was a logical question, he hadn't expected it. "I have my own set of–" He saw her gaze rise above his head and her eyes widen a split second before he felt the steel toe of a work boot in his ribs.

— . —

With the momentum of the blow, Luke rolled onto his side on the road. He covered up instinctively, continuing to roll onto his front and pulling his bent arms into his sides just as the second kick found his hip. His chin was on the asphalt, his eyes were on Colleen scurrying towards King Street as his ribs cried out.

Another kick into his right arm and side, then one into his left. He pulled his hands a little higher to cover his ears, fearing the next blow would be to his head. *Be a turtle*, he thought as more kicks landed, some partly absorbed by his shoulders and arms.

Then he got one right below his elbow and right below the rib cage. In the kidneys.

The blows stopped for a couple of seconds. "Where's ya money, wanka?"

"Give it up or I'll beat you to a pulp."

Then the steel toe found the side of his head, only lightly cushioned by the turban. He fought pain and nausea as he felt a heavy weight on top of his laptop within his backpack, probably two knees. Hands were going into his empty back pockets.

"Okay," he managed to say. He didn't have a strategy, but he knew the backpack was more important to him than the money. "I'll give it to you."

The weight on his back was removed. Slowly, painfully, he rolled onto his back. He saw a teenager standing over him.

"C'mon!" A kick landed on Luke's hip. He winced and stopped. He wanted to sit up but the pain in his ribs and arms was too great.

The kid looked over his shoulder for some reason and Luke heeled the kid's shin. As soon as Luke's foot came back to the asphalt it kicked straight up into the softness between the kid's legs. As the kid grabbed his groin, he yelled, "What?" before being swept away, landing with a thud on the pavement.

Gasping and trying to recover from the kick, Luke was able to open his eyes to see the kid lying face down on the pavement, his hands held together on his back by the homeless guy from Ravenscourt, Link. Except now, his knees were grinding the kid into the road.

"Yob!" he snarled at the kid.

Luke turned and looked the other way. Colleen was standing on the curb with her hands over her eyes.

After a minute, Link calmly asked Luke, "Did you lose anything?"

Luke moved his right arm enough to feel that his roll of bills was still in his front pocket. He shook his head slightly, unable to speak. What he really wanted to do was to curl up in the foetal position and take a near-fatal dose of painkillers. He managed to roll slowly onto his side, left ear to the road.

"Do you want me to tell someone to get the police or an ambulance?"

Luke shook his head slightly again and watched as Link allowed the kid to stand and kicked the staggering wanna-be-thug. Luke tried unsuccessfully to speak.

"You know where I live," Link said. "My shit's on the street, I gotta get back." He started to back away from the scene and Luke repeated his feeble nod of appreciation.

"Thanks," Link said to Colleen, as he walked past her.

— · —

Luke had to think. But his head hurt. *Get up!* he told himself. *You are lying on a road. It's the end of a cul-de-sac, but there are houses right beside you. There's a good chance the police are on their way.*

As he tried to pull his shoulders off the road, he could feel a thrust of pain where the first kick had landed. *You've had broken ribs before, and you survived*, he reminded himself. *They are going to get worse before they get better, so do it right away.*

He gradually curled to a sitting position, his arms at his sides. He stood up using his legs. His legs had bruises on the sides, but they were in much better shape than the rest of him. He looked around. He kicked the punk's black beanie-style hat towards the bushes at the end of the street. Bending over was painful to even consider. He kicked his water bottle so that it would roll to the end of the street as well. He looked back at the scene. Colleen was sitting with her hands over her eyes, non-functioning. The only other thing left was his own blood.

When he got to the edge of the bushes, he just sat down without trying to pick the best spot. He touched his head wound and it was bleeding alright. Like all head wounds it was bleeding enthusiastically, but head wounds were seldom as serious as they looked. He put a spare set of socks against it. Better to count on his immune system to fight the extra germs from the socks than to ruin his turban. Using his arms was painful. He'd wrap the turban around his head to hold the socks in place against the wound. Just the sight of him would probably trigger a call to the police.

His next instinct was to go to Ravenscourt Park. That's where Link was. Link was safety. But he knew that was wrong. He had to get back to his camp. *Is it safe to walk the footpath that would take me to the underpass of the M4? Is the punk really gone? Are there any other options?*

CHAPTER 5:
Tuesday

He was lying on his back with his laptop held against his chest, still hoping for some sleep. Getting the backpack off had been terrible, but he needed the aspirin inside it more than anything. He had used almost all of the water in his water bottle to wash his head wound. As his body stiffened, his ribs became worse and worse. He had broken his ribs once before, after going over the handlebars on his bike. Now they hurt whenever he took a breath, and he knew it would get worse. His arms and shoulders and hips were sore and bruised, but he was used to that type of pain after numerous hockey injuries that had never properly healed. The pain where the boot had struck was now acute. The thought of moving made him wince.

It must be blindingly early, he thought. The lack of road noise meant he had no distractions from his pain. Since it was already a new day, did that mean he should take his daily limit of aspirin now? It was tempting, but deep down he knew it would be wrong. And it would also require him to move.

He had always felt safe in London. He held London up on a pedestal really, relative to the other cities he had lived in. And now, even this one safety had just been taken from him. It felt cruel. It felt that, for reasons he couldn't begin to fathom, he was being punished every way a man could be. He was half-starved and filthy. His children would think that he was a terrible man, a thief and a liar. The horrible things that he and his ex had said to each other in the throes of their divorce, would now be believed. Having worked like a dog his whole life, he was now completely and totally destitute. And he'd be pissing red for the next two weeks.

If he survived that long.

For the first time in a very long time, tears rose in Luke's eyes and he didn't have the strength to stifle them. In the darkness, he sobbed himself out. And it hurt. It hurt his ribs, it hurt his breathing. It just hurt all over, inside and out.

The blaring horn of a large truck awoke Luke to daylight. He hadn't felt himself fall asleep and was a little taken aback that he had. The painkillers and the body's own need to heal had probably sent him off. Thank God. And the desperate need for more pain medication was probably what had woken him up.

Putting the turban on was painful and particularly difficult, as was checking in the mirror to make sure there were no blood stains visible on his head or neck. He eased himself out of his tent, his muscles screaming and his head aching.

By sitting with homeless Colleen, did he put himself in a position to be beaten and then robbed?

Homeless was just one letter away from hopeless. Nobody thought of a homeless person's waking hours as similar to a person who wasn't homeless. Instead, homeless implied despair, and a state from which there was probably no recovery.

Normally, Luke's confidence wasn't fragile. He didn't wallow in setbacks. But the question of whether or not he would ever throw in the towel was lurking in his subconscious. How long would he carry on like this, trying to sort out the mystery before he gave up?

At some point in the near future his roll of cash would be gone. What would he do then?

Would his family come looking for him? If they did, how would he know?

Could he subject himself to a long trial and a longer prison sentence?

The questions were like hammers to his already-beaten psyche. He couldn't answer any of them at the moment. No wonder he couldn't make any headway with the file. A huge part of his energy was grappling with the ugly reality of being a hunted homeless man. His reality was cramping his IQ.

He was not set up to be homeless. He had no experience with the underbelly of his own society. The homeless were people he walked past, occasionally shaking his head in sympathy but rarely-if-ever doing more than that. Never in his most terrifying nightmares did he ever envision spending his life washing himself in a restroom, eating his dinner outside, no matter the weather, and holding his hand out in the hope that someone more sympathetic than he'd ever been, would drop a fiver.

He felt tears prickling again. Partially it was rage that he had been brought so low after such a good life. Mostly it was fear. An almost paralysing fear that this would be his reality for the next few decades. If he survived that long. He would have to spend those decades with one eye cocked, looking for a killer. Looking over his shoulder. Being hunted like an animal.

After a while, Luke lifted his head. *Let's get going. Enough of this.*

He thought he remembered seeing a water fountain next to a building, and it was visible as soon as he exited the bushes. He shuffled towards it very slowly. But he was moving. Thankfully, the fountain was still working. He refilled his water bottle and an old food container he had found that might just prove watertight.

As he walked back, he saw a newspaper on one of the benches he was walking past. He told himself not to stop, but his eyes were drawn to his own picture above an article on the back page. Among other things, the article revealed that Luke Smith was an ice hockey player. A policeman stated that he had watched ice hockey on TV and believed it was a very violent game. He felt Smith could be a dangerous criminal and encouraged people seeking the reward to talk to the police immediately and to avoid direct contact with Smith if they encountered him.

He didn't feel very dangerous right now. He put the paper back on the bench, but his eye caught the picture on the front. There appeared two people he least wanted to see: Drinkwater and Braun.

Drinkwater was a force, a charming front man with cold eyes. Braun was something else again.

Luke and Braun had developed a mutual respect based on their interactions. Braun recognised that Luke knew what the real issues were, and Luke recognised that Braun was the mastermind of all things within BMI. At one point, when Luke had brought up an unresolved topic for the second time, he remembered how Braun had looked deeply into his eyes and said:

"You are relentless."

Luke knew that – at one point – he had been. He had been tough. Braun was not the first to describe him as relentless.

Last night had been a kick in the teeth in more ways than one. Now he felt as broken and vulnerable as, well, some homeless bum shuffling to a public fountain for a drink of water, frightened of a couple of teenagers.

This cannot continue. This has to be resolved. Something has to change. I have to find the solution. Something else has to give. I am not going to live the rest of my life like this. It was a resolution so loud that it felt like a bell sounding. *I am* not *going to live the rest of my life like this. I am NOT.*

It sounded simple. But in that simple decision was an inner core, now strengthened.

He'd once stumbled across the expression "sleeping rough" in an article on the lack of affordable housing. The expression meant just sleeping any place you could lie down. A fair few people who lived outside London chose to "sleep rough" in London during the work week. It allowed them access to London's better-paying low-to-middle level jobs, while avoiding the high cost of accommodation. Public lavatories interspersed around London and its mild climate were invaluable for this strategy, the article had pointed out.

Luke liked the expression "sleeping rough". And the more he thought about it, the more he liked it. It implied you were enduring your nights, but your days could be pretty much the same as anyone who slept in a proper bed. It sounded like something that could be overcome, could be tolerated or was simply a personal choice. The word "rough" was just one letter away from "tough."

He was a tough rough sleeper. Not a hopeless homeless.

As a relentless tough and rough sleeper, what should he do? Luke stared at the water, mulling it all over. He had options. He could walk away from this whole mess. He had just enough money to go places and do things. Maybe he could join a commune or do some field work, picking tomatoes or strawberries or whatever was needed. Then take his earnings and slip out of the country. He could search the internet for a way to contact his family without triggering the police. Maybe get a fake passport and go back to America.

And then what? Show up at his children's houses?

He let his mind linger on that. The greeting. The love. The joy. Dad was back! And then having to sit them down and explain to them the real truth. And deal with them insisting he go to the police. And him insisting that really, it wasn't worth his life and his time. Not without some understanding of what was so almighty important about this file that had accidentally landed in his inbox.

The risk. It kept coming back to that. As a risk manager, there was an irony of this being his situation rather than something he analysed.

Do assassins have passports and work internationally? Almost certainly yes. Is there any reason why the killer might let this one go? Almost certainly no. Would there be a risk to his children and newly arrived grandchildren? Almost certainly yes.

Then that option was off the table. No sneaking into the USA.

Really, what he really wanted to do was to figure out the file and get his life back. There was no other genuine option on the table. He had the Polish Centre and considerable anonymity. What he was doing was already the single most viable method of regaining his life.

Sure, he'd been beaten. But only physically. And once he swallowed some painkillers, even that wouldn't matter so much.

It seemed he'd arrived at a decision: figure out the file and how to survive the streets. Fail at either one and he was goner.

Luke knew that the resolution of this nightmare boiled down to a battle between himself and Braun.

And Braun was right about one thing. Relentless, that's what Luke was. He was relentless.

— · —

Zofia was sitting at her kitchen table, working to determine Smith's financial situation without much success on her WFH day.

It was wonderful to hear her hubby Petr come through the door. His eyes went to her laptop in the middle of the kitchen table. He then slowly and deliberately turned to look at her knitting project which was on the arm of the couch. There were only a handful of new stitches in it.

"A couple of stitches of rest and relaxation, I see," he said sarcastically.

She smiled and rolled her eyes as he leaned over and kissed her on the forehead.

"Hey, I made it to the Polish Centre right before closing

to post more of my help wanted posters. I've got enough work right now for more workers and I never know when one of my guys is going to decide to try and find work for himself."

"You can't knock that," she replied. "That's what got you where you are today."

"That place has been a gold mine for me." Petr paused and stared into the distance. "I remember clearly meeting a tall skinny girl there when she was taking a break from Jazzercise class to go to the water fountain."

"I wonder why I forgot my water bottle that day?" she said, standing up.

"I think the English word for it is *Cupid*." He put his hands on her shoulders and kissed her on the lips. He let his hands fall straight down until he was touching the bump that was more obvious every day. He kneeled and kissed the bump.

"And now," he kissed her again, "I have a beautiful goddess." She giggled and gently pushed him away.

Zofia clicked on an email from Maria. In it were a half-dozen call transcripts that the data science algorithm had identified.

None had the word *kidnap* in them. The first two were disappointing. The reports described objects that were being grabbed or pushed as part of theft reports. Obviously, the algorithm had determined the words *grabbed* and *pushed* were relevant and had flagged the calls. The third one was very interesting. She read it a couple of times and then put her headphones on to listen to it:

I noticed a minicab screech to a halt at the corner. It wasn't just the sound of the brakes, but I could smell that the tyres had skidded. You don't normally hear or smell skidding tyres. A man jumps out and runs into the Bureau de Change. Nothing too weird about that I guess ... some people need money fast. Only a few seconds later, much too fast to have done any sort of transaction, the same man comes back out and appears to be holding a man and pushing him into the minicab, which hasn't budged. The man is resisting but they both ended up in the minicab and it sped away, squealing its tires again.

Her mind was racing. There were no other reports of people going missing that day, she had checked that already. The time of the call was a little after Smith had interacted with the homeless man in Hyde Park. This was just what she was looking for!

— · —

"Tell me again what this is." Vicky asked as she, Jane and Fiona sat down in their usual spots around Vicky's small kitchen table.

"It's a weekly podcast called "Two Sides of the Story" and if you don't follow this, you've been up in the clouds somewhere, Jane exclaimed.

"With no time to look down," Vicky added with a chuckle.

"These two guys pick a topical issue and debate it. Politically, they are both close to the centre, but one, Liam, is on the left side, and the other, Henry, on the right. There's almost always some overlap between politics and business, so I think you'll like it. It's very popular."

Vicky's brow furrowed. "And two bottles of wine will get us through this?" She didn't have many female friends; she didn't know that many women. How odd that now, of all times, she was making female friends.

"More than enough," and they clinked glasses.

"Evening folks. No debate this week over the perfect topic for *Two Sides*."

"Yes, it's not often we commoners get to join in the hunt for a criminal. But it seems we're not very good at it," added Liam.

"No worries, Liam, I'm sure after tonight Luke Smith will come forward just to correct some of the ridiculous statements you make."

"No doubt. So then let's leave aside all of the ineffectiveness and issues within our policing forces. That's been covered. Let's chat about this entity, British Mutual Insurance, whose attempt at an Initial Public Offering is behind all this," Liam responded.

"Yes, and I think the underlying issue is the form of this beast, the *mutual* insurance company. It's a dinosaur, and the sooner we can demutualise, as they say, all of the dinosaurs, the better. There will be messiness along the way, and we're seeing some of that right now, but this form of company is a beast from the 1800s. We Brits aren't good at moving on from our archaic, comforting, legacy institutions. Why can't we make this an exception?"

"Henry, you never see the value of anything that provides a common good to the common people. These institutions need to be well managed, and it's not clear that BMI is. That's the issue with demutualisation, not the form of the beast," Liam answered.

"Well, I see this as no different from the Post Office fiasco. These quasi-public companies, which are neither fish nor fowl, are not properly run because their structure and mandate are ambiguous. Are they trying to make money by providing a service, like any other business? If they're not trying to make a profit first and foremost, then are they providing a public service first and foremost?" Henry paused. "That ambiguity leads to mismanagement. Who's in charge? Where does the buck stop?"

"You know, your rant doesn't surprise me one bit." Liam cut him off so briskly it sounded as if the lines were planned in advance. "The common element that pushes these things sideways is greed. There's no reason that the BMIs of our world can't go on doing what they've been doing, filling a public need and slowly accumulating profit as a result. It's the thirst for immediate personal profits that push these things sideways. You could see it as clear as day with other demutualisations. Management and the private equity vultures were clearly in it together from the beginning. There was no attempt to mask that at all."

"I disagree that this is just about greed, Liam. You could see it with that Building Society we discussed recently. When they have a windfall, they don't even know how to give it back. That's a problem of not knowing how to run these strange beasts that are still wallowing around in our financial system," retorted Henry.

Henry kept going. "Don't forget, it was blind trust in an internal IT system at the root of the Post Office debacle. Here it's an IT thing as well. Our legal system just assumes that if it came out of a computer, it's correct. Did you see the report that some of the systems that pay pensions are more than forty years old? The National Audit Office figures we can save twenty billion by improving our IT systems. And when do you ever hear a company come forward and say they're sorry, their IT programmers screwed up? No, it's some independent source that starts as a voice in the wilderness. What do you want to bet there's a screw-up in an ancient IT system involved in this?"

"Okay then, speaking of betting, let's put ten quid on what happens to this scoundrel," Liam offered calmly.

"I say he shows up in some alleyway pretty soon. He sells the data and then the folks who bought the data decide there's no need for this nerd to be at large any more. Ironically, the mortality thief becomes a mortality statistic, and humanity is better for it."

The three women all leaned back in their chairs, their eyes widening. Vicky couldn't bear to hear the rest and punched the mute key.

— · —

Drinkwater burst into the meeting room's open-air space. "Alaistair," he said, right hand extended, left hand clutching a pad of paper and pen.

Amber leaped to her feet. "Amber Leung." She looked him straight in the eye and tried to match the strength of his handshake. She'd put on some makeup knowing she would be going up to the executive suite but had strategically worn an old-fashioned and modest skirt.

"I couldn't help but overhear parts of your conversation earlier." Drinkwater nodded his head towards the open-plan meeting space where Amber had met with the eating club's chief actuary. "I hope you will excuse me for that."

Amber demurred politely. Alaistair Drinkwater was giving her the once over and Amber wasn't beyond being appreciative about it.

"Tell me about your work."

It was the textbook open-ended question and shame on her if she couldn't nail this one.

"It's challenging. The firm gets paid by the hour, so we are incentivised to maximise hours. But the good thing about consulting is you tend to see the company's problems and help to fix them. You get to work with all types of companies on all types of products. And with all types of people."

"You must be top drawer to make it all the way up here, to this floor, from Hong Kong. You're brave, outspoken, young and ambitious. You're all the things that our actuarial team is not. We have the classic chicken and egg problem. Our actuaries can't attract actuaries who aren't like themselves. That leaves the rest of us to take that situation into our own hands."

"Wait a second, are you interviewing me then?"

He nodded.

Her heart sped up. This was timely. *Perhaps I should move from consulting to BMI, especially now that it's going through a very lucrative IPO. Money attracts money.* Her parents would like that.

"I'm sure you didn't come with a CV, but if you'd like to proceed, tell me something that you've discovered which no one else has. Something that really makes you stand out."

Alaistair just wanted a bird. He watched her sifting through her experiences, searching for something to impress him with, and suppressed a smile. She was young and pretty. And very hungry. Foreigners always were. Especially those from dictatorships. He knew how it would go. They'd have a night or two of fun. If she transferred to BMI, he'd put her with a good team, which she would take as a commendation, then work twice as hard to prove herself worthy, and in the process, genuinely earn her commendation. They'd part on happy terms.

So his stomach curdled when he heard:

"When I compare your mortality results to the industry's, they are close to the industry average for the last ten years. Or certainly within statistical variation. But within those years, there are a number of very bad years in the middle. And they are worse than statistical variation would allow."

There, she had played her highest card to get a new job, Amber thought to herself. Setting up a social meeting with BMI's chief actuary weeks ago, who also ran the dining club she had just joined, got her onto BMI's executive floor, and that was about to pay a huge dividend because she'd just hooked the biggest fish in the pond, if his dropped jaw was anything to go by.

Drinkwater blinked hard. "I'm interested." And he meant it.

"On the positive side, there's been a sharp improvement over the last few years, and that seems like a story you should want to tell. But there's also questions about the bad years that would have to be answered. Do you want me to go into the statistics?"

"No, no," he replied quickly. "It's too late in the day."

"Whenever I find something that I don't understand, that's when I dig the hardest to learn and understand."

"Who else back at your office is working on this mortality mystery?"

"We don't have access to any files anymore and everyone has moved on to other projects."

That's a damn good thing, Drinkwater thought. "But it's on your computer still, right? So I can look at it later?"

"Oh yes."

"Anywhere else I can access your analysis?"

"Not at the moment."

"You okay to keep going over this at dinner?" He smiled and hoped it didn't look like he was baring his teeth.

"Yes, of course."

"I need to finish a couple of emails, and then I will head to one of my favourite restaurants." He scribbled on a piece of paper. "If you can get there in half an hour, I will be in one of the booths at the back."

Amber nodded.

"Oh, one more question. What would it say at the bottom of your CV, Amber? You know, personal interest, that type of thing?"

"I love playing rugby."

— . —

Drinkwater's limo pulled up alongside the near-identical limo in the far reaches of the car park. The only difference was that the other car had windows so black the limo could have been goth. Drinkwater got out, took two steps and got in the waiting car. It sped away.

"Thank you for seeing me," said Drinkwater.

The heavy-set man in sunglasses and a dark suit didn't respond or change his solemn expression.

"As you may know–"

The dark suit cut Drinkwater off, "I know your situation very well. Are you here to repay or are you here for more?"

"More. As soon as the IPO–"

The dark suit raised his hand and Drinkwater stopped mid-sentence. He raised his phone and started tapping on it. "Two years?"

"Yes," Drinkwater responded.

He raised his phone to Drinkwater, showing a number with a bunch of zeros. "You pay me back twice this in two years. No ifs, ands or buts."

Drinkwater nodded. "Thank you."

"And our current deal remains in place."

"Yes, the current deal remains in place."

The limos came together again. As Drinkwater reached for the door handle to leave, the other man said conversationally, "Just a second." He flipped another app on his phone and showed it to Drinkwater.

It was a live feed. Men in work gear, masked and goggled, were plucking bottles from stands and letting them drop on the brick floor. Smashed glass flew. The champagne sprays spun and sparkled like diamonds. It was methodical. It was work.

Drinkwater knew in a heartbeat exactly where they were: the temperature-controlled vault under his kitchen in the Cotswolds.

"What a shame," Drinkwater murmured.

"Yes, it is," the man agreed. "Better a bottle than your back."

Drinkwater gave his disarming smile, changed cars and drove off. But he still had a tight ball in his stomach and he consciously had to loosen his jaw. It was clenched so tight he wasn't sure he could slide a fork through his lips. The IPO had to go through. Otherwise, paying off his debt would save his back but liquidate every single penny he had. Everything. It would all be gone. The house. The other house. The ski chalet. The boat in the Caribbean. The antique cars. His wine cellar was already gone. He'd spent so much time and money on that wine cellar. He could replace that. He could replace everything. In theory. In practice, it would not be easy. If this IPO didn't go through, he'd be ... Drinkwater searched for the word that meant you had nothing ... *broke*.

— · —

The mortality results for ages above sixty were very close to industry levels, and improved across the ten-year period in a very similar way to industry results. It was the same conclusion as the results before the age of forty, which was really no conclusion. No story there, nothing for BMI to be paranoid about.

The results for males between ages forty and sixty were giving Luke a headache. They certainly didn't line up with the industry, so maybe he should be happy. But they were just plain confusing.

Ten years ago, BMI's mortality levels were in line with the industry. Then they took a steep turn for the worse over roughly a five-year period. They were so much worse than industry levels that something had clearly gone awry. Then, the results quickly reverted to being close to, or better than, industry levels. All within the space of the last ten years. He had even done the analysis in two-year age groups instead of five-year age groups, but this didn't shine any new light on the situation.

There was something lurking there, Luke knew it. He didn't have a specific hypothesis to test though. Maybe it was just as well, his laptop's batteries were as empty as his mental batteries.

However, at the end of day, that's what he'd discovered: a puzzle. It was something! He just needed to figure out how to peel that onion down one more layer. The faster he did that, the fewer the tears.

He crawled awkwardly into his sleeping bag, laptop on his chest. His ribs wouldn't let him forget that he was breathing. He tried to slow his breaths. He wondered what Vicky was doing. It was probably twenty years since they had worked together at Silverthorne for the first time. When they saw each other again after all that time, he'd commented that she looked great. Then, realising his misstep, he said he hoped she would forgive his comment now that she was his boss.

His comment had been sincere. He'd forgotten her striking

combination of blue eyes and black hair, with a figure like something out of the movies. As they worked together, he marvelled at how the eager analyst had matured into such a confident and effective leader. When the feelings had started to stir, he'd done his best to suppress them. At least until the team picture in the boat statue and then the rose incident.

After he and Vicky had parted that night and he got on the Tube, he started asking himself what he'd been thinking with the gift of the rose. He hadn't been thinking. Or rather, he'd been thinking with the wrong part of his anatomy. He certainly hadn't come to London looking for a relationship. Was he just reacting, as any warm-blooded heterosexual man would have, to the physical touch of an attractive woman?

No, he was a logical person, not impulsive. That rose was so out of character that it took him aback as much as it had Vicky. Maybe that proved something special had happened that night?

From where he lay now, in a sleeping bag on top of some leaves and twigs, he wondered why he hadn't bought all the roses in that damned shop for her.

— · —

"Okay ladies, we've been through the story of the rose, the weekend footie is well behind us and Luke Smith is still at large. The calendar yawns. We need something to work on." Jane moved restlessly in her clothes. She was used to more action than this.

Vicky and Fiona moved towards her, agreeing with her through their actions.

"Guessing you have an idea," Fiona replied as all three sat with their wine glasses.

"I certainly do," Jane snarled. "Over the past couple of years, we've all seen this Post Office meltdown. A once-respected organisation puts in a new IT system – that has glitches."

Vicky, who knew something about IT systems, wanted to interject and say: IT systems don't have a glitch. They have "issues" which need resolution. But she held her tongue and listened to what the policewomen were saying.

Jane continued. "Only no one knows it's the IT. And those who do know, aren't saying. Instead, the bosses accuse a whole bunch of innocent people of stealing money. People go to jail. People are ruined financially. People commit suicide. The Post Office denies it for as long as possible. Been called the greatest legal travesty of all time."

"Amen," Fiona declared as Jane paused to take a sip of her wine. Then Fiona added, "Now a mutual insurance company is hyper paranoid about something that came out of its IT system. You heard it on the podcast, there are parallels."

Jane frowned in concentration. "The Post Office didn't have any stolen data which it reported to the police. The Post Office actively covered up what was really happening. By going to the police and offering a reward for its retrieval, BMI is doing the exact opposite."

Fiona was also thinking aloud. "But what if BMI is also engaged in a cover-up? The bigwigs know that the system doesn't work and that this will affect the share price during the public offering. Somehow Loverboy Luke (Vicky rolled her eyes at that one) gets hold of the data that proves that the system has errors. The police are called to get that file back because it's the only proof. When the bigwigs get the data, they'll bury it again. The IPO goes through and they make a ton of money and Loverboy goes to jail, just like the Post Office."

Both women swivelled their eyes to Vicky.

"There's lot of public information available about the Post Office Scandal and about BMI," Vicky said thoughtfully. "Let's get it all out here on the table and see if we can find any connections. I'm certainly willing to divulge anything I know about BMI to you policewomen to help solve a crime."

— · —

Drinkwater's eyes opened suddenly. Had he actually fallen asleep?

Dinner had been average. The wine above average in quality and quantity. His dessert, lying next to him, absolutely delicious. Amber's beautiful naked body was nestled against his. His left arm was under her neck. Her eyes were closed. She had a slight smile on her face even in her sleep, as if she was dreaming mischievous dreams.

He hoped it was still early. If he could get out of here and get home in good time then maybe there could be a double feature that night. He lifted his left wrist to see the time. Her eyes opened slowly. Her smile grew.

"Hello beautiful," he whispered. She turned her face to him. He could see the work of the wine in her sleepy eyes.

He waited a few seconds. "What are you doing tomorrow night?" He stroked her cheek with his right hand.

She paused while summoning the ability to speak. "Eating club with a bunch of stuffy actuaries."

"Where and what do stuffy actuaries eat?"

"Italian place on Bayswater. By the park. Should be done by eight." Her smile was wide now, and her eyes were perfectly focused on his. "Why do you ask?"

"I'd say our first little rugby match was a high-scoring draw. We'll have to keep playing."

CHAPTER 6:
Wednesday

Luke's eyes opened to pitch black. He thought of Vicky's hair. How he wished he had woken up staring at it, their bodies spooned together.

He was still on his back, but his laptop had slid off to one side. The pain of breathing wasn't any better. But there was a new pain this morning – hunger. So this was what it felt like to wake up hungry. It was a totally new feeling for him. He'd been a hard-working man, but he'd also been a lucky man. Every day he was learning that lesson again and again.

He crawled from his tent and got to his feet as soon as he noticed the tiniest bit of light in the sky. He wasn't quite to his feet when he stopped cold, and fell back down to his ass in fear. Six feet from him was a man. How long had he been there, completely quiet? Luke thought of his money. It was in his pants which were in the bottom of his sleeping bag. The silhouette of the person, the light of the street behind him, caused Luke's blood pressure to come down slightly from its all-time maximum. There was no mistaking the shoulders and hair. It was Link. But was it crazy Link or functional Link?

"I know who you are," Link declared quietly.

The ache in Luke's stomach became a twist. Luke just didn't know what to do. He couldn't physically run. And he wouldn't leave his computer behind. There was a moment of stunned silence. Then Luke spoke.

"I'm not a bad person. I'm trying to solve a mystery so that bad people will be treated as they should be treated and good people will be able to live their normal lives."

It didn't sound convincing even to Luke. Link didn't react to the statement. The silence was drowned out by the morning's song. Eventually, Link turned and walked back towards the motorway. Luke watched him, still at a loss to know what to do.

Then Link stopped and turned. "How do you like it here?" His head turned each way, an estate agent valuing a property. "I stayed here for a while at first. Eventually the traffic got to me. Otherwise, a nice spot." Luke wouldn't have been surprised if he'd said, "Location, location, location."

Then Link turned and walked away.

Luke held his head in his hands. Even that movement was physically painful. Mentally it hurt that his personal fortress of leaves was no fortress; it was practically a half-way house for the homeless. *Would he ever feel safe here again? Would he be able to get any sleep here? Was Link his ally or about to collect the bounty?*

It was a bad start, but he still had to make the most of the day. He started at the lamppost and looked west. He had been hesitant to go west because to go west was to walk through a narrow lane. The signpost instructed cyclists going west on the path that they must dismount. There were a couple of large metal posts positioned at the entrance to the lane to make it almost impossible not to dismount. Part-way down the lane, there was a sign that said The Dove, which he had noticed the other times in the morning when he had looked down there. He was certain that it was a pub.

He needed a new path to the street to avoid any thugs and Colleen. While he didn't blame her for distracting him and he appreciated that she'd called Link for help, she was still not getting a Christmas card from him this year.

So he went east. Walking hurt, but he knew it would help his eventual recovery. The path along the river remained wide and deserted as it passed under the bridge. As Luke got closer, he got a sense of how massive the two supports that went into the water were. From the side of the bridge, they had looked surprisingly narrow. After passing under the bridge, he paused to see its eastern side. It was lit dimly but directly by the rising sun. It was a magnificent structure.

A group of joggers, some with headlamps still burning, came towards him. In a moment of panic, he ducked into a set of narrow stairs that rose to the roadway over the bridge. He climbed the stairs. As he got close enough to the road, he paused and looked both ways. There were two pedestrians walking on the side opposite him and he paused to let them go by. A similar set of stairs led down from the other side of the bridge and he walked across the road to them. The stairs were as cramped as the ones he had just climbed, but they descended to a different part of the area - to the end of a narrow road, not to the wide paved path along the river.

He went down the stairs and followed the narrow road to its end when it made a left back towards his camp. So far, he hadn't encountered anyone. Given how the rest of the area was waking up – dogwalkers and parents with children were filling the open spaces – the quiet at this end took him aback. He just wasn't sure if this made it safer or more dangerous. *I guess I'll find out.*

— · —

Zofia hadn't slept well, and the early start of her day had been predictably stomach-churning. As soon as she got to the office, she went directly to her boss. He listened in silence and then said, "Okay, go to the conference room and get the witness on the phone. Ping me when you get him on the phone, and I will join you."

During the call, the witness repeated the details in the transcript accurately. Zofia asked for more detail about the man being pushed aside with no success. They asked whether there was much time between when he saw the incident and when he called it in, and he said he had called it in right away. Just as they were about to end the call, the witness volunteered some additional information.

"A couple of other bystanders and myself watched the cab speed away. You don't normally see a cab being driven that way. Not too far down the road, the cabbie jabs on his brakes again, with the screech as loud as his first stop. The business-man comes tumbling out of the cab onto the street, and the cab speeds away."

Zofia's heart sank with the longer description. Apart from that, this was perfect support for her kidnap theory. On hearing the description of the victim getting kicked out of the cab, her boss let out a huge sigh. His expression and body language changed to one of disinterest. "There you go. Someone got robbed on Friday. You should investigate THAT," he said as he walked away.

She sighed. She'd got him involved too early. She wouldn't make that mistake again.

— . —

That day, Vicky made blueberry pancakes for the three of them for breakfast. The table was covered with two printer cartridges worth of stories on BMI and the Post Office Scandal. So far there had been no breakthroughs. Breakfast, which had been served on top of the pages, was halted for a press conference on the case.

Alaistair Drinkwater stepped up to the microphone. His height and square chin gave an aura of authority. His hair was perfectly coiffed and gelled that day. He wore a charcoal-grey suit with a white shirt and patterned light-blue tie. There was a pin on his lapel displaying the BMI logo.

"Today, the reward for information leading to the capture of Luke Smith, and the return of BMI's precious data on death claim beneficiaries, has been increased from twenty to £100,000." He pronounced the number very slowly and emphatically. Then he paused. "This is because our first priority at BMI is protecting our customers." He paused again. "Our partners at the Met have confirmed they can offer amnesty to anyone who has been harbouring Smith."

The press smelled blood. "Can I clarify!" called a man in a suit, looking very distressed. He inserted himself in between Drinkwater and the microphone. He explained that amnesty was too strong a word and went into the legalities in excruciating detail.

"Have you had ransom demands for the data?" A reporter demanded. Other members of the press started to blurt out questions and jabbed their mics closer to the podium to catch the answers, like fishermen stabbing with spears.

"Sorry, no questions at this time," the representative from the Met asserted and walked away, only to be followed by the majority of the press.

The three women looked at each other, appalled by the stakes going up. That kind of money changed people. They would take risks where none was called for. They would get aggressive when they didn't have to. It made it more difficult for the police to do their job and more dangerous for Luke, wherever he was.

Vicky began slowly thinking aloud. "When I was last home, I was looking at our family picture at my sister's wedding. Her life's not perfect, but she is very happy. And here I am, working so hard, waiting for some polo-playing guy with an impressive accent and a country estate and a wine cellar to sweep me off my feet. My ridiculously expensive dating service gets me the odd guy who says he wants to date a banker, then bails when he discovers bankers actually work long hours. Lately all I've been getting is the odd Wednesday or Thursday date, none of them amounting to anything. And I look at Luke helping the analysts on the team the way he helped me twenty years ago and I think, *What am I waiting for?* It feels like a shout, not a thought. When we have the closing dinner for this deal, I know whose arms I will be in that night."

Fiona looked up at the ceiling thoughtfully before intoning, "Flirty financier falls for mortality mercenary. A Mills and Boon bestseller."

Even Vicky had to laugh at that one.

— · —

Luke still had a puzzle on his hands. Which is exactly what he'd been looking for.

His instinct, as always, was to keep drilling down, getting to the next level. After yesterday's findings, the next level would be to break those male age forty to sixty results down into what were known in the insurance business as underwriting classes.

Underwriting classes were first introduced when the huge difference in mortality rates between smokers and non-smokers became evident. Premium rates for new policies were raised for applicants in the *Smoker* "class" and reduced for those in the *Non-Smoker* "class."

In his working career, he had seen first-hand how the industry reacted to the AIDS epidemic by requiring a blood sample from applicants. Collecting blood had slowed down the underwriting process, but all of the information collected in a blood sample quickly demonstrated the link between health markers such as cholesterol levels with expected mortality rates. Additional underwriting classifications such as *preferred* and *non-preferred* became common. This fine tuning of who was at higher or lower risk meant that policy holders didn't subsidise each other.

So, while he had identified the overall trends over the past ten years in the male aged forty to sixty range, he would have to determine if this class was driven by incorrect underwriting.

If one class of policyholders had been subsidising another to a large degree, that would be embarrassing to management.

Would that be enough to kill for?

— · —

Zofia's boss clicked on the "play" icon and the two sat uncomfortably closely to watch the video.

"Some camera on King Street in Hammersmith picked this up. My buddy sent it along because there's a bloke with a hat covering his ears. Thought we might want to take a gander," he explained.

They watched in silence as a tall skinny kid with a black hat that covered his ears kicked a guy on the ground in a turban. Zofia tried not to wince or show emotion with each blow. She squinted to try to see the faces more clearly.

"That's not your Mr Smith right," her boss said, pausing the video and putting his finger on the skinny attacker. "He's older and some sort of executive type, right?"

"He's certainly not a tall skinny kid," Zofia replied, hoping her tone didn't sound condescending to her boss.

He hit play again and they both straightened up when another man suddenly entered and subdued the attacker.

"Do we know who that guy is?" Zofia asked.

"Yes, a homeless man. Lives in Ravenscourt, loiters in front of the Polish Library, which is close by on King Street."

"Should we talk to him?" Zofia asked, realising she had probably put some zlotys in the guy's jar at some point. She kind of recognised him.

"We have in the past about other incidents but he's off his meds. Those types are rarely coherent."

"What about the Hindu guy? He must have shown up at a hospital somewhere?" Zofia questioned. She had learned that often crimes were not reported because the victim didn't want to draw police attention to themselves. The silence that followed her question told her that she could do that if she thought it was a good use of her time.

Eventually her boss spoke. "He's probably illegal. Maybe he'll take the hint and go back home."

— · —

Drinkwater was alone in his office when his personal phone vibrated.

"You're all set my friend," the voice on the phone said confidently.

"So, you've … I mean he's …" Drinkwater didn't know how to ask the obvious question.

"You aren't going to see a headline and you don't get to see a body part in this business."

"Well then. What's done is done," Drinkwater said, composing himself.

"We don't know if he did anything with the data before we got to him," the voice added. "It's impossible to know that. But there's no reason to believe he did. All our sources were a chorus on that matter."

"Like a chorus of angels, I'm sure." Drinkwater's voice was now rising in jubilation.

"You'll make sure the transfer goes through promptly?"

"I'll pop the cork as I do."

"Cheerio." And the call ended.

Manny had got to where he wanted to be by hard work. Slogging through endless practice tests for the 11+ exam, his father slapping him across the face every time he got a wrong answer, had given him a bursary to a posh school. By the time he sat the exams, he wasn't bruised or blackened. It had worked out well for both Manny and the school, a success story to bring a tear to the eye of every Guardian reader: poor boy, given a chance, achieves.

Manny did well enough at school, better on the rugby pitch

where the full contact suited his compact and muscular body. He did better still at footie, where he deployed a cunning level of viciousness.

His teachers, watching quietly from the side lines, propelled him into the military – officer class. The pay was too low for Manny. And there were too many restrictions. So he got out. Then came the scramble to make a living. A short stint in prison had reinforced what his dad had always said: *Got to be on top – or else.*

He had contacts. He'd been beat up for as long as he could remember. He was well trained in hurting and killing. He put it all together and opened a security firm.

Mostly, he beat the crap out of people to get them to do things. More thug than hitman, although clearly he was multitalented. Mostly he worked for drug dealers and payday loan sharks. It was nothing too big, not the mob. Besides, organised crime wouldn't take a veteran. He'd been surprised by Drinkwater's first "contract" years earlier. That guy really wanted his ex to be six feet under. Silly cow. He was astounded that his high-profile school roommate was a repeat customer.

He knew there was risk in asking for full payment when he had no trace of Smith. But there was a cashflow problem. Life in London did not come cheap. At this point the most likely scenario was that Smith would not come forward. Wherever Smith was and whatever he'd done with the data, he was gone, as in gone gone. And given that the guy knew an awful lot about something very bad, the pencil pusher was going to stay gone. Manny wasn't as smart as these guys, the Drinkwaters of the world. But that's what even he would have done: gone, never to be seen again.

So Manny figured that he might as well claim the reward. Drinkwater could afford it. And this payment would allow him to sort a couple of things out. And besides, he'd keep looking. This wasn't over. Not by a long shot. Let's call this payment ... a deposit. And as a reward, he'd been given another task. Also lucrative. And undoubtedly easier.

Manny took undiluted pleasure that so many people had cheated Drinkwater: his wife, this pencil pusher and now him. Unlike the pencil pusher, Manny had given himself a lane to do the backstroke if the data ever got out. He'd been smart enough to do that.

He was taking a big risk, but then, he was in the risk business.

— . —

Drinkwater called Braun using his personal phone to pass on the good news. Drinkwater sat quietly in his big chair while the news sunk in.

A successful IPO and the riches it would certainly bring meant a bigger country home, with horses perhaps, another renowned golf course membership and a consequential donation to something prestigious. Most importantly and above all, his debt would be paid off. In full. Maybe even early.

Every muscle in his body relaxed, his jaw eased and he sank deeper into his chair.

— . —

Zofia's coffee was almost too hot to hold as she went back up Silverthorne's elevator to the designated interview floor. The one member of the IPO team who had been unable to meet with her earlier, Gabby, had become available immediately. She'd already finished typing up the rest of the reports, which had all sounded the same. Smith was a respected, hardworking expert and a great team member. Blah blah blah. At least Chief Inspector McConley could take the reports to MI5 as confirmation that Smith was possibly kidnapped, in the hope of getting the agency more deeply involved. So far, all they had heard from MI5 was that there were no reports from their insiders of the BMI data being up for sale.

Zofia took the biggest gulp she could before entering the interview room. She exchanged pleasantries with Gabby, nodded to the lawyer who looked even more blandly nice than he had during the interviews that morning and went through the disclosure of the recording.

"I understand you were the member of the IPO team responsible for the dissemination of all of the financial information between various team members."

"Correct."

"Can you please describe how the actuarial team was organised?" Zofia asked.

Gabby looked at the lawyer, who nodded slightly.

"Silverthorne hired one of the top-shelf actuarial consultancies. That's standard in a deal like this. They provide a number of people at different billing levels. In addition, Vicky Headley hired Luke Smith to be the leader of the team. The mortality experience was one of those areas where we knew we would have to answer questions, and that's why Vicky hired Smith. He had ultimate approval authority for anything with respect to the mortality results."

"Had Vicky and Luke worked together previously?"

"Yes, at Silverthorne years ago."

There was something about the lady's tone, something about the nature of the response that caused Zofia to pause and compose a question that she hadn't listed in her notes.

"Was there anything more to it than that? The relationship between Vicky and Smith, I mean."

Gabby looked into Zofia's eyes and nodded as the lawyer interjected, "Let's not go there."

Zofia's eyes narrowed momentarily. "That's all. Thank you very much." She stood up abruptly and offered her hand.

The moment the two of them left the room, Zofia pulled out a pad of paper and started scribbling:

Last Laugh Theory
Smith and Headley are brainy lovers

She puts him in position to steal

BMI is Smith's last gig (he is in his 50s!). This is his ticket
to Margaritaville. He gets payday AND gives the middle
finger to the industry. So he'll sell the data then disappear.
Headley will join him later.

She needed to get some estimate out of MI5 on what this
data might fetch in the black market. She could get some help
looking into Luke's finances. She bet he wasn't doing as well as
one might have thought.

She'd have to figure out how to reshape this to make it sound
stronger, more Met than a movie. And then she'd take it to Mc-
Conley. She could see the smile on his face already.

— · —

Luke squeezed his eyes tightly closed. *How could this be possible*,
he wondered? The results for the underwriting classes that were
riskier than standard were very close to industry levels consis-
tently across the ten-year period. Ditto for classes at less risk
than standard. The entire anomaly he had uncovered yesterday,
the bad results for five years, followed by five good years, lay in
the standard class.

So, BMI's underwriting methods were as effective as the industry's, except for a whole bunch of lives that had a high death
rate but were classified as standard.

He had expected the phenomenon of poor results for males
between ages forty and sixty to be spread across the underwriting spectrum. Once again, he should rejoice in having found
something unexpected. Except he was now left with a puzzle
within a puzzle.

A retreat to the park was all he could think of to somehow
get his head around this.

With his last few minutes, he searched for BMI on the internet, found a video about the press conference and clicked on it.

He jumped when he heard someone talking rather loudly in Polish behind him. He turned to see the lady from the reception area looking straight at him, talking sternly and tapping at her watch. He nodded as deferentially as possible and gathered his stuff into his backpack. She was clearly going to hover over him until he left. He was flustered, unsure whether to focus on packing up or on placating her with more bowing and scraping.

He had watched far enough into the press conference to understand that the reward for his arrest was now five times higher than it had previously been.

With this kind of money being promised, how much longer could he keep hiding from the world?

— · —

During his dinner at the river wall, Luke's attention was grabbed by groups of people coming out of the lane talking louder than they needed to. He reasoned that they were probably coming out of The Dove. In most British pubs, it was easy to drift outside with your beer. It was not unusual to see people simply put their beer glass down and walk away. Often there were beer glasses that had been left on the wooden picnic tables outside The Rutland Arms and The Blue Anchor when he looked towards the bridge first thing in the morning.

He looked down the alleyway to The Dove as he walked past it on the way to his camp. Something very bright caught his eye. As he moved a bit closer, he could see that someone had left a half full beer glass on a window ledge about ten yards from the near end of the lane. The sun's light was refracting through the glass in an odd, alluring way.

He walked quickly to the glass, picked it up, walked even quicker to the near end of the lane and ducked behind some bushes against a house. The bushes were taller than he was. He hadn't given any of this a second's planning. If he had, he would have noticed that the bushes were thorny and he now had considerable scratches from stepping right through them. His ribs and upper body complained about his quick movements.

Between the bushes and the wall of the building, he sipped the beer, savouring the beer's warmth and bitterness. A couple of groups of people walked through the lane in the few minutes this took, no more than three feet away but oblivious to his presence. He could hear the chatter inside The Dove when the door opened, and he swore he could smell the inside: fusty and foody and the longed-for scent of human bodies standing close together. It was the best warm half-beer he'd ever had.

— . —

The target stepped out of the Italian restaurant on Bayswater Road that Manny had been directed to. She was the only Asian female to enter the restaurant, and she'd emerged alone. She stepped away from the door and dug out her phone. She tapped quickly, slid it away and gently weaved her way across Bayswater Road.

Perfect, he thought. *She's drunk.* As the target walked past him, Manny took a couple of quick steps to catch up and walk alongside her. It was only a few seconds before the woman looked sideways at Manny.

"My gun is pointed right at your head," he said, cocking the gun and pressing the muzzle a little harder against the inside of his jacket with his right hand.

The woman recognized the distinctive sound of the cocking pistol. Her expression instantly flipped to terror.

"What ... what do you want?" she asked, voice trembling.

"I'm going to put my left hand on your shoulder and we're going to walk casually together across the street. We'll do our talking in the park. Unless you'd like this to be your final resting place," Manny put a vice grip on the target's shoulder. She felt more muscular than he expected, but she was clearly intoxicated.

As they entered the darkness of Hyde Park, Manny grabbed the woman's right hand with his left and pushed it up the woman's back, causing her to gasp and hunch as they kept walking. He heard the phone fall to the ground from her left hand. Manny forced her towards the denser section of woods that he had scouted that afternoon. He pulled the woman's other hand behind her back using both of his gloved hands and pushed her down to the ground onto her chest and face. He jumped on the woman's back, positioning his knees to break ribs on both sides. He held both the women's hands together with his left hand, pulled the gun out of his jacket with his right hand, dug the end of the silencer into the backbone and pulled the trigger. He wished it was Smith.

The force of the bullet caused the woman's chest to bounce slightly off the ground. As Manny got off the target's back, he stuffed the gun back in his coat and scanned the area carefully to make sure that no one had seen. When he was sure that the coast was clear, he walked back to her fallen phone and slipped it into his pocket to break into later. She did not have a computer. The bullet fractured the seventh thoracic vertebra, nicked a large blood vessel and tore through lung tissue on its way through the target's body and into the ground. She felt intense pain in her back and chest but had no feeling below her chest. Within seconds, she was unconscious. Within minutes, she was dead.

Manny didn't wait for the final breath. He bundled her into a large wheelie suitcase he'd hidden in the shrubs nearby, and strolled to the road just like any other man in expensive dressy-casual clothing coming home from a trip. There was a waiting taxi and he got in, lugging his bag with him. Serene as could be. The taxi drove away.

—— · ——

"Someone steals your Rolex, The Met will run 'em down," Jane said without emotion. A number of empty wine bottles now held all the pages on the kitchen table down.

"Someone steals money out of your bank account, we've got a cybercrime unit for that," Fiona added.

"Someone screws with your finances in a way that's a little bit under the surface ... we've got nothing for that," Jane said.

"Maybe we should all go to night school for financial modelling, and we'd have that covered," Fiona added, her glazed eyes rolling.

"In theory," Vicky chimed in, "auditors should catch numbers that don't add up. But the only maths I've ever seen them do is billable hours times billable rate equals what you owe." Vicky had joined the griping.

The three women were exhausted, the two policewomen were confused and alienated from all the numbers. In comparison Vicky was frustrated to the point of screaming. Taking all that into consideration, a good wallow in their misery was not wholly unreasonable, indeed, it felt therapeutic.

"I'll start again tomorrow," Vicky assured them. "But for today, we're done."

—— · ——

When Luke got back to his camp minutes later, he considered what had just happened. Had his impulsiveness been driven purely by his thirst for beer? Or was he doing the only thing he could to associate himself with the enjoyment other people were experiencing? Pleasure by osmosis. He had never really been deprived of things that others around him had, so was he just reacting the way a needy human would in the same situation?

Regardless, he'd just acted homeless. There was no doubt.

He had just put everything at risk for no good reason. He didn't have the luxury – if you could call it that – of indulging in homelessness: nicking beers, begging for spare change, stinking to high heaven.

The sense of disquiet deepened into something else. It wasn't just the scoffing of the beer. It was something deeper than that.

It was how very natural it felt. It felt automatic. Like, that was how he was meant to live. Against his will, to his complete and utter astonishment, he was turning into a homeless man.

It terrified him.

CHAPTER 7:
Thursday

It had been as easy to break into the cheap housing as it had been to break into the phone. *Really, they should make these more resilient,* Manny thought, as he donned head-to-foot hazard-protective gear, and even that he did while already well covered in sterile plastic. The police would be all over this place and he had no intention of leaving a trace.

Her place was neat and tidy. The computer was evident. He picked it up and slid it into his hazmat bag by the door. Then he methodically looked under the bed and through the cupboards, every place there was to look. But nope, that was only that one computer. He did however take the stacked bundles of American dollars hidden in the top drawer. He considered that rightfully his. As fair payment for a job well done.

He had a phone call to make and an invoice to submit.

— . —

Luke woke to the memory of the previous night. When he started to move, he was reminded of the beating. *He must be improving,* he reasoned, *otherwise he would have been aware of the injuries before he moved.*

"I'm getting there," he muttered as he levered himself vertical. Then he savagely thought: *No mumbling aloud! Rough sleepers don't talk to themselves. Act rough, not homeless.* First thing a rough sleeper does is get well and truly clean. Maybe he could get some soap and then jump in the Thames, scrub himself with sand, scrub his tee shirt and trousers. What the heck, why not buy a new tee, socks and underpants?

He was at the river wall in time to watch the sun start its climb through Hammersmith Bridge. He could do it now, before anyone came. The tide was a bit low but it was quiet, with just enough light to see. Luke peered around the wall, looking for a place to clamber down easily.

On the near side of the river, on the sand that was exposed by the low tide, there was a body.

Blinded by the sun, he walked quickly east along the path to get a closer look. It appeared to be an average-sized woman, wearing a dark business suit, lying completely still and face down. His eye was caught by the handbag, bumping gently on the sand next to her, its long strap wrapped up and over her shoulder. *That probably meant that foul play was not involved*, he surmised.

Luke's mind got stuck on the handbag. Handbags had purses. Purses had money. He could go down there and get his hands on the purse pretty quickly and pretty easily. He could take the money out in a couple of seconds. *Should I just keep the handbag?* He wondered. It would offer a new identity, even if only for a short period until this person was found to be missing. He could get some form of transportation, maybe a bus or a train. Would that inevitably leave a trail to wherever he went?

Do it. Do it now, he told himself.

He swung his left leg up onto the top of the wall, bouncing on his toes to get the other leg over. He could feel the bruises on the outside of his legs and around his ribs. Then a sudden flash of light caught his eyes. A boat speeding up the river had a light on its roof. Luke pulled his leg down so quickly that he tumbled to the base of the wall. Then he crouched behind it. Someone had seen the body and called the police. The boat landed on the sandbar ten yards away from the body, its wake dislodging the body from its resting place. The side of the boat said *Marine Support Unit*, with a coat of arms beneath it. It was very likely that more police would be there very soon.

Staying was high risk. Luke scrambled to his feet, hurried back to the camp at breakneck speed, ignoring the painful complaints of his battered body. Once there, he rushed to hide everything much more carefully than he normally did. Then he sped off.

He felt like smacking himself up the side of the head. His impulsiveness that morning was even worse than his impulsiveness the night before outside The Dove. What the fuck was wrong with him?

— . —

Luke walked the same route he had taken the morning before. There was little, if any, human activity on King Street at this time of day.

He walked past the Polish Centre. It didn't seem the same without people. He noticed stirrings inside the bakery, but the Medjool Market was dark and still. He decided to come back in a couple of hours.

Ravenscourt Park also felt very different from when he was last there about a week ago. The only human activity was that of the homeless. He picked a bench in the southernmost end of the park, shrugged off his backpack and started to take out his laptop.

Then he stopped. What incorrect, time-sucking hypothesis was he going to test today? For the first time since all of this began, he had no plan on how to solve the mystery. He sat and considered that.

Then he realised he was angry. At himself and at the world. He couldn't figure it out. What the absolute fuck was going on with this file? Near as he could determine, literally nothing was out of the norm. But clearly something was, otherwise BMI would not be offering £100,000 for him and the data.

He was so frustrated that he wanted to punch a wall. Or better still, a person. Or even himself.

The thought ended when a new smell reached his nose. A plan was hatched within seconds. *Wait, is this just today's version of smelling the beer outside the pub?* He asked himself. *No,* he decided after carefully considering it, *this plan isn't as self-indulgent.*

— · —

Luke walked gingerly up to the part of Ravenscourt Park where he had first encountered Link on the day of the head injury. He stood at the edge of the path. There would be no surprises this time.

He held two small brown bags with grease stains. Each one held a fresh muffin and a fresh croissant from the bakery on King Street.

"Hello!" He called out. "Hello, it's Luke." He choked on the last word as he spoke it. He doubted anyone heard, or that if they did, they would have understood it. Nonetheless, he turned to walk away, perhaps even run. But it was too late.

"Hey, good morning!" He heard from behind him.

He turned around. Link looked down at the bags and said, "My favourite bakery. Why don't you come on in."

Link moved expertly around some bushes and Luke tried his best to mimic the moves. They arrived at the large tree and Link motioned that Luke should sit, which he did. He handed one of the bags to Link, who then sat on the opposite side of the tree.

They ate in silence for a couple of minutes before Link asked, "How are ya feelin?"

"I'm okay until I breathe," responded Luke. "But getting better."

There was another period of silent eating before Link spoke up again. "I have anxiety ya know, but they've never really come

126

up with a diagnosis for me. I've heard bipolar, I've heard anger management, I've heard just about everything over the years."

Luke heard a bit of pride in Link's voice that he defied consistent categorisation.

They both finished within another silent minute. Luke was happy with silence. No questions about his wardrobe. In the silence, Luke suddenly spoke. His words surprised him. "I'm not sure I can do this. Like any of this. The violence. The hunger. The fear … I saw a dead body this morning in the Thames. Just floating. I keep trying to talk myself into this being something other than what it is. But …"

Luke's voice trailed off. The image of the body, bumping against the strand on the ebbing tide, swam unwanted around his head. He was a statistician not a mortician. He was supposed to meet mortality through data, not in the flesh.

The silence just sat there. It was as if he hadn't spoken. Did he mention the dead body? Christ, but he hoped he wasn't going to cry again.

"I'll see you back on King Street by the Polish Centre," Link stated.

"Yep, thanks again."

As Luke got up, he noticed that Link hadn't touched the muffin. Surprised, his eyes lingered on the bag.

"For a friend," Link explained.

— · —

During the search of Furnivall Gardens, one of the more junior policemen had seen Luke's tarp and waded into the bushes for a closer look. It was clear to him that someone had spent time there. He radioed his supervisor:

"I've found a tarp in the middle of the brush. Has grommets and appears fairly new. Can't see any rope in the area. Should I bag it?" He asked. "Oh, and it smells like vomit back here."

"Some poor sod is probably going to be returning to it and sleeping under it. Stay close enough that we can talk to whoever is calling it home," was the response.

He backed out, going right over the buried luggage and large backpack on his way out of the woods.

— · —

"Hey there, Bumpy, still trying to help you on Smith," Maria began. It was Zofia's first call of the day, which was a good thing, given how much of the morning she'd spent hugging the toilet and then making herself something to eat. Rinse and repeat.

"I *am* reconsidering my statements on naming rights for the firstborn."

Maria chuckled. "Wait till you hear this. I was able to do a wider search for Smith's name on that Friday. Not just our records but all emergency services. I ran it last night. Took forever, but our CPU would have otherwise been idle."

"Okay, okay. Give it to me. I've got knitting to do you know."

"Ha ha. Smith was a first responder on an ambulance run in Hyde Park that morning." She paused as long as she could stand to let it sink in. "Turns out he was an EMT in the States years ago. He came into St. Mary's in an ambulance with a patient who was having seizures."

There was silence.

"So, he had some time to kill before the big heist and thought he would help his fellow man. Just like the average criminal," Zofia responded in a sarcastic tone. "That's awesome. You'll get the Nerd of the Month parking spot for that one."

"I think that one's reserved for pregnant ladies now."

"In all seriousness, thank you, Maria."

"Over and out."

Great, she thought, *just what the case needs, one more data point that makes Smith seem like a very unlikely thief*. And it blew her romance theory out of the water. She was back again to Smith being kidnapped. She decided to figure out a way for Maria to be the one to explain this finding to Chief Inspector McConley. Maria certainly deserved the credit and the exposure.

— · —

"Need you on another case. You can go back to the homeless stakeout first thing tomorrow."

The cop in Furnivall read the message and started to move. The park was a nice break from his normal day, but he was certainly getting bored.

— · —

At lunch, Amber was still working, but couldn't resist checking her phone. *Had there been any follow-up on the topic of the rugby rematch?* Nothing. *Had she and Alaistair even exchanged numbers?* She couldn't remember; there were fuzzy parts of that evening. In fact, everything that happened after she walked into BMI's building seemed so crazy. *Did it really happen?*

There was a text last night from her friend and co-worker, Xiaowei Deng.

"Hey, you envite me to this dinner than don't even show? WTF? These ol farts are actually funny when they're dunk. U still owe me."

Amber had forgotten that she'd invited Xiaowei to the dining club last night. Her bad. She did owe Xiaowei. She'd been really tired and hungover yesterday but had intended to go to the actuarial eating club that evening. It was her night to meet the higher-ups, play the game, get herself known. But it hadn't happened.

She had stretched out on her sofa for a power nap, setting her alarm for seven o'clock, which would give her just enough time to fluff her hair and get to the dinner. But she'd forgotten to change AM to PM and had slept through to morning.

She grinned to herself. Wednesday night with Alaistair Drinkwater, handsome CEO, had been worth it.

"Let's study together tomorrow. I'll buy lunch," she texted back. Actually she hadn't that much work to do. And Alaistair was very interested in the work she was doing on the mortality statistics. It was also quite the puzzle.

She put her real work aside and opened her computer to the file of data she had on the mortality. *Let's figure this one out,* she thought happily to herself. *Compliance be damned. When I show him the numbers, that'll really knock his socks off.* She gave another silent giggle.

— · —

As soon as Luke crashed through the bushes once again to his camp, he could see immediately that the tarp had been moved. There had been disruption. He had the feeling of his house being broken into.

Everything was still there, he quickly determined, and there was no evidence that the suitcase had been dug up. If it wasn't a dog, it had to be a human. One of his biggest fears was that another homeless person would find his camp and ransack it. He was starting to understand why you often saw them carrying all of their possessions with them all the time.

He felt even more nervous about the location of the camp. He'd already done some exploring to the east. It was now worth doing some more exploration even further west.

He had planned to move quickly through the narrow lane and the entrance to The Dove, but his eyes wouldn't let him. A sign indicated that the words of the song *Rule Britannia* had been penned there by James Thompson in 1740. There was also a poem:

Children may not come inside
Although an awful lot have tried

Come inside yourself we plead
But keep your dog upon a lead

His mind was pulled to his children. But this was the wrong time for those thoughts. One of the first houses on his right had an unusual sign on its wall. The sign declared that this was The William Morris House. Luke didn't recognise the name, but he was curious enough to stop and read the rest of the sign. Morris was a designer and craftsman, poet, printer, socialist, novelist, environmentalist and idealist. *Quite the CV*, Luke decided.

Luke was turning to walk away when a poster next to the fixed sign claimed his full attention. The society was having a talk next Sunday: *Utopian Dreams and Ruskin's Tory Paternalism*. It was part of a series of lectures on John Ruskin and William Morris. Apparently, Ruskin and Morris had a significant influence on each other, even though their political views differed by one hundred and eighty degrees. Luke didn't know anything about Ruskin's political leanings, but he recognised the name.

Of the ten actuarial exams that Luke had passed back in the day, one was on calculating and analysing mortality rates. Luke had a perfect picture of the textbook's cover in his mind. It was red with gold lettering with a graph of a smooth curve on the front. The curve showed the number of people assumed to be still living for each successive age. A large portion of all actuarial maths was derived in some way from this curve.

The book's first page – before the Table of Contents – held a quote from John Ruskin. Luke remembered it still.

The work of science is to substitute facts for appearances and demonstrations for impressions.

The quote was probably chosen to help convince the reader that what they were about to learn was indeed science. So this is where the guy came from. London. And he was pals with all-round-genius William Morris. Go figure.

It depressed him beyond words. He wasn't up to their standard. He would be quoted in no one's textbook. No lectures would be given about him except as a statistic, a drop in the ocean of homeless people.

His lips twisted bitterly. He wasn't sleeping rough. He was homeless. And he was even bad at that.

CHAPTER 8:
Friday

The process of "scraping" data from real-world sources for autopilot analysis by countless artificial intelligence algorithms continued its 24/7 grind. At some point very early on Friday, the data from a video camera located in the Polish Centre's art gallery made it to the top of its queue. It was then analysed for matches to facial and gait recognition data that had been separately collected for selected people.

— · —

Jane saw the post soon after it had been put up and called her supervisor immediately. She knew that if Vicky saw the news, she and Fiona would have to resuscitate her.

"It's certainly not him," her boss reassured her. "We don't know anything about who the victim is, but it's a true statement that it's not Smith and there's no reason to believe it's related to Smith. We're going to put that out ASAP."

By including the words "body" and "Smith" in its news release, the Met's story took on a viral life of its own.

— · —

Alaistair Drinkwater's heart was racing that morning as he got up to his maximum speed on the treadmill. His heart rate jumped to its absolute full capacity when his phone buzzed, the story came up and his eyes were drawn to "body" and "Smith."

His legs froze and he was immediately launched off the treadmill across the room.

He distinctly remembered the phrase "would never be seen or heard from again." A dead – not disappeared – actuary could also mess up the IPO. Ignoring the pain in his body, he scrambled for his phone, the sweat making it hard to press buttons. Soon he realised that it wasn't Smith's body which had been found. It was a young Asian woman, not yet identified.

His heart rate came quickly down. He gave a skeleton smile.

— · —

Manny was driving Simon's minicab again that day. Luke Smith was like a loose tooth his tongue couldn't stop poking. *He's gone, gone, gone.* It was a mantra that he kept repeating to himself. But it didn't calm him down. Manny wanted closure. He wanted certainty. He wanted to well and truly kill the bastard himself now. Driving the minicab was meant to get his mind off all this, but it hadn't worked yet.

He'd just dropped a customer off on Chiswick High Road when the hat caught his eye. It looked like the floppy hat that Smith had purchased back in Hyde Park. A small lady was wearing the hat while pushing a shopping cart very slowly. He parked his cab illegally and jumped out to walk alongside her. "What a lovely hat," he started with. "My mum is always in her garden. I'm sure she'd love a hat like that. Where'd ya get it from?"

The lady seemed to pay him no attention. Then she stopped. "Charity store on the high street ... just there." She said, nodding her head across the road.

"How long have you had it?"

"Picked it up on the weekend. Just started wearing it yesterday ... 'pends what else I'm wearing, ya know," she said looking down at her clothes and at her wardrobe layered into her cart.

"For twenty quid it's yours dahlin'... cheapest gift for your Mum you'll ever find."

Manny turned and jogged back to the cab.

Instinctively, he had known that Smith had gone west after he put his phone on an eastbound bus. He was certain Smith wasn't in Ravenscourt Park. He pulled up the map of the area to see what other green spaces were close.

Manny didn't see any homeless people in or around the small park on the north side of the river, Furnivall Gardens. The bushes were very dense, just like on the other side of the river. *They would provide good cover, if he were trying to hide,* he thought.

The tarp caught his eye as he peered into the bushes. He pushed in and a sharp branch poked him in the shoulder.

"Fuck!" he exclaimed when he saw the tear in his jacket. It just wasn't his day.

There was nothing unusual about the campsite. He'd seen others like this. No personal effects, so it might be an old site, or its resident might be out pushing their shopping cart around.

— · —

Luke had been searching for another starting point, another hypothesis on why BMI didn't want anyone looking at the details of the death claims they had paid. After a couple of hours he had something that he thought was a legitimate possibility. He remembered reading that BMI's longtime CEO had died about five years earlier. That's when Drinkwater was brought in and the momentum towards the IPO had started to build. *Maybe BMI had paid a huge death claim to the former CEO's estate?* CEO pay attracted a huge amount of public attention, but some sort of "death bed" policy, or maybe a series of policies would be a very effective under-the-radar way to pad his estate. It would be the type of thing that would show in the claims file but nowhere else, and the type of thing BMI would be extremely embarrassed to describe. It would be consistent with the mortality results he had found for standard class males. It was perfect. *Why had he not thought of that before?*

The only problem was he couldn't remember the previous CEO's surname. He sorted the claims file alphabetically by beneficiary, and headed to the library to find the surname.

— · —

Jocko was proud to be a part of the team that day. The men had done another cleanup in Ravenscourt, and the reporters they had invited were very happy with the pictures and quotes they got. The editor of the paper was a supporter of the cause and had come to the camp, offering his support after the scathing article that had appeared in another paper. They had all agreed that an article emphasising everything good would be best.

Jocko knew this was a use of precious goodwill. He also knew the men were disheartened after their high expectations of the Smith reward money. Billiards and a darts tournament, with hors d'oeuvres, was the solution.

Jocko had served in Afghanistan with the man who ran McMasters. He had told Jocko to bring his group there any time he wanted. If Jocko could split the cost of the food with him, and split a tip for the waiting staff who wouldn't get any drink orders while the veterans were there, the owner would be glad to have them. Jocko knew this was an expenditure of goodwill, but with the men disheartened by the lack of progress on the Smith hunt, it was the right time to draw from that reserve. The Treasurer of their group agreed with Jocko that it was a timely move.

The men were astounded. Billiards, darts and hors d'oeuvres! Those words weren't in their vocabulary.

— · —

Manny got the news relatively quickly because he monitored the progress of the investigation.

He hadn't known the name of the young woman he was supposed to kill. It affected him not in the slightest that she had been identified and the next of kin contacted.

His phone rang. It was his old schoolmate. Manny answered it with a smile of self-congratulation on his face.

Then his ear blistered and the smile ran off his face.

— . —

Amber's smile couldn't have been broader when she agreed to meet for a quick drink with her new lover. "I'm working on something to show you," she told him as the lift slowed to her floor. "I'm a little stuck with some of the coding so I probably won't complete my analysis until later – then I can tell you."

— . —

Luke stepped into a cool, clear evening with a full moon becoming clear.

His most recent hypothesis had been a dud. The prior CEO had a policy that paid a couple of million. No headline there. Nothing that would explain the mortality puzzle for forty to sixty-year-old males. Another waste of a day.

As he walked towards Cromwell Avenue, he could hear someone talking into a microphone inside the pub on the corner. The wide doors to the pub and the windows were open. He slowed down to listen.

"I'm sure you'll recognise this next ballad after a few bars, it's one of me faves. *The Streets of London*," the guitarist said as he reached to adjust some of his equipment. Luke knew this song. The first words and notes pulled him back to much younger days when it had been one of the closing songs at an Irish bar he'd frequented. It pulled him back to five or ten years ago when Annie Lennox had made it a soft hit again. He had a bit of a thing for her and liked much of everything she did and sang and said and supported. Talk about reach. One song, written by someone unknown, affected millions more. And it was about the homeless. How many pop hits highlighted the bums of the world?

As the song ended, Luke started to sing it to himself, "in his eyes you see no pride –"

"'Scuze me mate."

Luke jumped as he realised someone was talking to him. He turned towards the speaker who continued, "The lads and I continue to hunt for that public enemy with the gnarly ear. Would ya mind confirmin' you is not he by liftin your headwear for one second? Please sir."

Men wearing military fatigues were closing in on him with billiard cues in their hands, their eyes fixed on his turban, sounding aggressive and demanding.

The decision was primal, quick and instinctive.

He took one large step towards the group and swung his backpack at them, barely clipping the man who asked him the question on the chin. The men in the front lurched backwards, knocking those behind them off balance.

Luke turned and ran. His head start was a couple of seconds, and he was sprinting like he'd never sprinted before down the middle of Cromwell Avenue while struggling to get his backpack on. In hockey, it would have been a breakaway. *Everyone's chasing you. Keep your focus on technique,* he told himself, *there's no advantage in thinking about the players chasing you.*

The reality was that he would have to win not just the 100-yard dash to the end of Cromwell Avenue, he would have to win the 400-yard run and perhaps the mile as well. The prize wasn't a ribbon, it was freedom.

He could hear the men yelling as they ran behind him. After making the slight turn onto the path at the end of Cromwell, he ran towards the subway that went under the motorway. He was following the route he knew, but he knew he shouldn't lead them back to his camp. His legs, his lungs and his ribs reminded him of how long it had been since he had done anything like this and how recently he had taken a beating. He could tell from the sound of their footsteps and their yelling that he was increasing his lead. He had won the hundred, and he might win the mile, but other people were probably seeing this spectacle. As soon as someone realised men in fatigues were chasing a man in a turban, they'd call the police immediately or intervene directly. He wasn't going to escape simply by running faster than they could.

Luke emerged from the subway and ran on the pavement alongside the motorway, right past his camp. He made the slight turn into Furnivall Gardens and peeked to see that his lead was about 50 yards, which was still close enough for them to see each turn he could make. He ran along Rutland Grove and turned right onto the short street in the direction of the base of the bridge.

As soon as he made the turn, he slowed down just enough to take his backpack off, struggle with the top of a commercial lidded bin and toss his backpack in. It was worth giving up a few seconds and the risk of the metal scraping sound as the lid opened and closed. The laptop couldn't go where he was headed.

At the bottom of that street, the path ran straight into the river. They'd see him turning left onto the stairs up to the road over the bridge. He was counting on that. He took the stairs two at a time. When he got up onto the road, he ran straight across it to the narrow set of stairs down the other side of the road. The road had a fair number of pedestrians on it. He would be out of the sight of his pursuers when they got to the top of the stairs, and he was counting on them assuming he would go across the river on the bridge or, at a minimum, pausing in confusion.

From the bottom of the stairs on the other side of the road, Luke ran straight towards the river, veered slightly to be underneath the bridge, knocked his sunglasses off and tried to execute a track-and-field-style triple jump. As he ran, he jumped with his right foot, planted his left on the front edge of the river wall, then planted his right on the far edge and pushed off as powerfully as possible. His legs kept moving as he became airborne, and his arms swung like he was trying to fly. His eyes were locked on the water.

In the split-second before he hit the water, he noticed how beautiful it was in the moonlight.

— . —

The vets followed the stairs up to the road across the bridge and continued across the river, just as Luke hoped. Once they got to the other side of the bridge they slowed up. They were running among pedestrians now, and many of them were still holding their billiard sticks. They hadn't seen Luke since his turn up the stairs. Roughly half of the original group were no longer with them, either unable to run that far or unable to deal with the anxiety of the situation. The remaining group paused and decided quickly to disperse into four groups of two or three people each, one turning left into the Harrod's Village area, one continuing straight on the same road, one turning right into the wooded area next to the Thames and the last doubling back over the bridge. They would meet up at the same spot in ten minutes if they hadn't found him. They wouldn't tell anyone about their chase or whom they had discovered.

— . —

When Luke hit the water, he had his feet wide apart, and his arms outstretched. He wanted to go underwater but not too deep. As he submerged, the instantaneous sensation was one of comfort. The weightlessness reminded his body and mind of the start of a triathlon practice swim, and the feeling of flying. More importantly, he was out of sight.

Then the saltiness of the water, the pressure on his bruised ribs and the complete lack of light reversed his comfort. He felt like he had already done a triathlon. Now he needed to do another one.

His immediate plan was to get to the far side of the first supporting column of the bridge. By staying under the bridge, he couldn't be seen by anyone on the bridge itself. By getting behind the column, he wouldn't be visible from the river's edge. He came up for a breath, looked for the column and swam underwater until he reached it. He came up for another breath that would get him around to the far side of the column.

He treaded water for a few seconds to catch his breath. The turban had come off the instant he hit the water, and he checked that it wasn't wrapped around him in any way. The water was cold and the power of the tide pushing him upstream was surprising. He took a deep breath and swam diagonally upstream and towards the houseboats while staying underwater. He hoped that with the force of the tide behind him he could make it there in three breaths.

In the darkness of the night, Luke couldn't see anything when he was underwater, and he wasn't even really sure when he was about to surface again. Having his shoes and clothes on made him a very inefficient swimmer. When he came above the surface for his second breath, he could see that he was getting fairly close to the houseboats. He realised he would now have to swim by braille, making sure his hands were always a little bit ahead of his face. He didn't want to crash into one of the hulls face-first.

He touched a hull just as he was coming to the surface for the next breath. He swam a little closer to the pier, putting himself between two boats. He couldn't feel his feet. And when he put his hand on the hull, he couldn't feel the metal of the boat.

Hypothermia.

He had to pull himself out of the water and up onto the pier. But if he pulled himself out here, it'd be right in front of everyone sitting at the picnic tables outside pubs. If he swam upstream to the pier outside The Dove pub, he stood the chance of being detected by houseboaters, though not an audience of beer drinkers.

With the help of the current, he got to The Dove pier quickly. Luke could feel himself getting numb, the deadening effect of the water moving up his torso.

What he had forgotten to visualise about The Dove pier was that there was little to no light from streetlights. After another very cold ten seconds of swimming close to the boats, he saw an area on the side of a boat where a ladder could be attached. There was an indentation in the hull that turned out to be large enough for him to be able to get a two-hand hold.

He reached up and grabbed. He forced his fingers to close and his muscles to pull. From there, he was then able to pull himself up just high enough to reach one hand on to the top of the boat. He could feel his whole body shaking and his teeth were chattering furiously. He was perilously close to ending up back in the water.

His desperation helped him hang on and get his second hand up. He tried to swing his knee over the railing, but he did not have enough strength – his knee slammed excruciatingly into it. He couldn't suppress his scream as his entire body shook with pain.

His grip on the boat loosened and he felt himself slipping off. Luke knew that if he fell back into the water then he would not be able to get out again. Gritting his teeth, he summoned all of his strength to propel his body over the railing and collapsed painfully onto the deck.

Gasping for breath, he saw that the houseboat's cabin was completely dark. Some of the other houseboats had small lights on in the living areas, some didn't. He hoped that no one had heard his scream of pain. Forcing his aching reluctant body to get up, he staggered off the boat and onto the pier. As he made his way towards the gate of the pier, he saw a flashing light on a boat underneath the bridge moving quickly in his direction. Luke cursed and forced his heavy feet to move faster.

Just as he'd prayed, the gate could open for those leaving the pier without a code or a lock. As he exited the pier, he heard a voice from one of the houseboats immediately behind him. "Hey, hey you. Stop. Stop!"

He stumbled hurriedly along the path and past the alleyway, straight towards the motorway. He ducked into the brush as soon as he could. Once he was ten yards into the brush, he laid down flat, shivering, and pulled the leaves and brush over himself as best he could.

— · —

The veterans had reconvened as planned and saw the flashing lights of the *Marine Support Unit* boat. None of them had seen any trace of the turbaned Smith, nor anyone who seemed to be on the run. The reality was that if he had gone west into the woods by the water's edge, it would be impossible to find him at night. If he had gone far enough straight along the road, he would have reached the London Wetland Centre. It was very large so finding him in there at night would be a longer shot than finding a needle in a haystack.

The police had exited the boat and were now talking to people. The veterans got close enough to a few of the interviews to hear that someone had dived in the water.

They pulled into a tight group. They agreed there was a chance this person going into the water had been Smith. They hadn't seen him beyond the point where he was climbing the stairs to get to the bridge. It was possible Smith had drowned and they did not want to be associated in any way with Smith's demise. They would come back and scour the entire area at sunrise and get the reward that they had earned. They would go back to McMasters and settle up.

As the men dispersed, Jocko stayed behind. He remembered their last proper sighting of Smith and had his own strategy to find the fugitive.

— · —

Manny was sitting at a table at the front of The Blue Anchor when he saw the flashing lights on the river. He refused to rush out to see what the fuss was about, even when others did. He would have to delay his leaving until this police action was well past. Manny and the police didn't mix.

— · —

The members of the *Marine Support Unit* walked west down the river path towards The Dove pier. They had also received calls of an intruder from a couple of the house-boaters on the pier, and it was hard to imagine that this was not related to the person jumping into the water. There was no point in putting a diver in the water at night back where the person had jumped in. It had been clear in their interviews that the person had deliberately jumped in, not fallen in. While it was still possible that the jumper had drowned, it was less likely than if it had been an accident.

— · —

Luke was still flat on the ground in the bushes. Shivering a bit less now, he felt that he could continue to lie there a little longer. He could see well enough out from underneath the bushes to watch the police moving towards The Dove pier. *Stay still,* he told himself, *wait until all of this dies down before you move a muscle.*

— · —

Jocko remembered that Smith had been carrying a backpack when they'd first confronted him. But when he caught a glimpse of Smith making the turn up the stairs towards Hammersmith Bridge, the backpack was gone. He was pretty sure that he was the only one who'd noticed that. Finding the spot on that street where Smith had hastily stashed the backpack was going to be the key to finding Smith.

— · —

The police met at the gate to the pier. They had a short conversation, and two of them proceeded onto the pier, out of Luke's sight. The two other policemen headed back towards Furnivall and turned on their powerful flashlights. One made a turn down the alleyway towards The Dove and The William Morris House. The other was walking directly towards the bushes where Luke was lying.

Lie still, he told himself again. *Unless that cop shines his flashlight directly on top of you, there is no way he will see you.* It was hard to override his primal instinct to get away and ignore his need to move for warmth. The policeman came to within a yard of the brush and walked close to the edge while shining his flashlight in. Luke held his position facedown right against the ground and stayed completely still. His heart was still pounding from the swim and the cold, and it wasn't slowing. It thundered in his ears so loud that Luke couldn't hear the cop leaving and only barely noticed the light moving down the lane.

Luke waited for all four of the police to leave and did his best to wait for a few more minutes after that. His EMT training told him to warm up right away, any way he could. He stumbled back to his camp through the bushes, which was no easy feat. It was almost impossible to see anything, plus his muscles were frozen and stiff. First, he found his headlamp. Then he checked the pockets of his soaked pants for his roll of banknotes. As he feared, the roll was gone. He cursed.

When he put dry clothes on, he breathed a sigh of relief. He felt so much warmer, so much calmer, so much safer. Sadly, he only had one pair of shoes, and they would be soaking wet on his feet for a while. He wished he had the turban, or even the floppy hat, just for the warmth it provided.

Without his turban and sunglass, he felt naked. Though slightly warmer now, especially as he began walking slowly towards the bridge, Luke still felt like he'd been beaten up by the chase. Every muscle in his body ached agonisingly. When he got back to the dumpster, he paused, looking up and down the street. It was dark and silent. Not a soul in sight. It was weirdly quiet – no movement or noise. It was as if the world had gone still. Waiting.

He couldn't see into the dumpster because of the hinged lid, but he remembered he had put the backpack in the front left corner. Bracing himself for the inevitable stench, he lifted the lid and reached in. And touched warm flesh.

As he yanked his arm out, he felt the strap of the backpack against his arm.

Without a moment's hesitation, he thrust his hand back in and this time, his fist punched and grabbed the backpack.

And started a tug of war.

Blood pounding, Luke slammed his left hand down, close to where his right hand was holding the strap of the backpack. He felt his hand hit someone's face and poke them in the eye. The blow caused their hold on the backpack to loosen, and Luke managed to pull the backpack out to the top edge of the dumpster, but a hand continued to grip it.

Then he began to lose the tug of war, with the backpack moving back over the top of the dumpster. The other person was better braced, leveraging their feet against the inside of the container. And they were just plain stronger.

But the backpack held Luke's freedom. He wasn't letting this one go. He brought his full weight to bear on the straps. Slowly, the backpack inched in his direction.

When his adversary's hand got to the edge of the dumpster,

the lid suddenly came slamming down on the hand. The grip released and muffled howls of pain began. Luke tumbled backwards, still clutching the backpack desperately, his momentum slamming him to the ground.

Luke sprinted to a nearby street corner, not looking back. Then he slipped between some houses, slumped against a wall and slowly slid down it.

It took the man a few minutes to get out of the dumpster. Luke could hear the cursing and his steps as he walked towards the houses Luke was in between. Luke wanted to pull his legs in a little more but found he couldn't move. Luke's mind was in overdrive with anxiety, and his body seemed to be frozen.

The man walked past.

Still Luke remained frozen, like a fly on flypaper, exposed to the most casual of glances.

Eventually, the man came back and went in the other direction from the dumpster.

Luke sighed with relief.

— · —

Jocko's left hand was throbbing excruciatingly. He could only move his fingers a little, and it was so painful to do so that he didn't want to try more. He had gone in every direction from the dumpster and had seen or heard no trace of Smith. As he sat down next to the dumpster, he wanted to cry.

He'd been so happy with himself for finding the backpack.

— · —

Luke hobbled back to the camp with his backpack securely fastened to his body. He knew he had to move quickly but it felt like he was trekking through treacle. He just couldn't seem to function.

A swim in a river and a tug of war in a dumpster. From which he'd emerged still functional. Physically, at least. He was still battered from getting beaten and cold to his core. But physically, he was more or less unscathed.

Psychologically, however, he was very scathed.

This is why the homeless move so slowly and look so confused, he realised. If they weren't broken by the time they start, then they would be a week later.

There was about five hundred pounds or so still stashed in the backpack. He opened his suitcase and dug out his alternative disguise. He really wasn't sure if this would work – he hadn't even tried it on. But there was no other alternative at this point. The man from the dumpster was no doubt still in the area, so Luke wanted to get on his way quickly. The homeless Sikh living in this site would now officially disappear, never to be seen again.

"Not so fast, Mr Smith," came at Luke from behind. He turned to see the back-lit silhouette of Jocko, one arm in an improvised sling, no more than ten feet away.

"You won the race and you won the arm wrestle, but you won't win the war."

Jocko didn't sound threatening, but he had the air of someone who would not stop until he got what he wanted.

Luke was at a loss for words. He thought he could win another foot race if he had to. "I didn't know that was you, back in the dumpster." He thought some more. "It's my backpack, you stole it."

Jocko remained calm. "I found it in the dumpster. Didn't seem like you wanted it anymore."

Luke had gathered himself and was ready to reason. "You know why I put it in there and you probably know it's the key to me proving I'm not a criminal. And you, for one, should know I am not the criminal type."

There was a silence. Luke wondered if he could simply grab what he needed and exit the bushes at speed in the other direction. Up from nowhere, a question burbled.

"By the way, how is the gentleman who fell on the park bench? He gonna be okay?"

— · —

An email arrived in Zofia's inbox from the Met's IT department titled, "Call as soon as you wake up."

— · —

After the handshake agreement, Jocko went back in the direction he had come from. He'd been given some pain medication by Luke and swallowed it immediately.

Being outnumbered, he hadn't been in much of a position to bargain. He knew that someone somewhere was watching. Because Luke Smith had had both his hands wrapped around the straps of the backpack. So who'd slammed the lid down on him? Jocko was pretty sure that Luke hadn't even considered that, despite his big brain. Or maybe he just wasn't as familiar as Jocko was with the heavy metal tops of large bins. They didn't just fall. Or get lifted off again a little later. But why was Mr Invisible playing hide-n-seek? It made Jocko twitchy, like he was back in Stan.

But he had a small core of satisfaction. He'd found the guy with the turban. They'd fought. He'd dealt with his extreme stress. He'd got his act together enough to make a deal.

If he hadn't been in so much pain, he'd have grinned in triumph. Maybe once he got the money, he could consider other options. Maybe he was on the road to something better.

About that deal. He'd made his call to Manny before he'd found Luke. So that agreement back there in the woods – it was moot.

— · —

After the handshake, Luke crept off, hunched and shuffling like he was much older than he actually was. Or homeless.

He couldn't detect the eyes that were fixed on him.

He just walked. And walked. And walked. It wasn't a march or a quick step or even a stroll. He'd have to pick up the pace to match Simon and Garfunkel's *Slow Down, You Move Too Fast*. His mind was blank. He couldn't think of anything at all. It was as if the Thames had washed his brain clean of everything.

And still he walked. Or shuffled.

If asked what he was feeling, he'd have struggled to find any emotion besides a longing for his little space in the bushes at Furnivall Gardens. In hindsight, it seemed snug, almost homey with all the amenities: the river in the morning light, the roses in bloom, the fabulous architecture of that bridge, The William Morris House with its lectures on Ruskin, The Dove pub with the occasional beer.

It'd been pretty good there.

But mostly he just walked blindly. He couldn't even decide on the path. His feet chose for him. He couldn't process anything. The only thing he could do was put one foot in front of the other. And so he did.

He was on the fringe of Bedford Park now. He used to live here, at one of the very first suburban developments in the late 1800s, famous for its architecture. He remembered the feeling of walking home from the Tube after work and retraced those steps. *There is no better icon of my textbook career*, he thought as he stared at his reflection in the large street-level window of his former home, *than this moment*. Then he realised that the police might have some sort of surveillance. He forced himself to move on.

He walked for hours. Finally, he allowed himself the luxury of sitting on a street bench. There were few, if any, cars on the road and no people. There was nothing to see. And nowhere to go. There was nothing to think. He had failed to find out why the file was so important. So he just sat. His mind empty. His soul emptier.

He was an analyst who couldn't analyse. This experience had been a giant failure of analysis. The best part of the past few days had been a stolen half-beer and the kindness of the Polish at their community centre.

His whole life had been built on a house of cards, on the shaky assumption that his ability to analyse could solve the problems that confronted him. What an egotistical, self-indulgent and narcissistic sham.

He wasn't an analyst. He was a fugitive. He wasn't a rough sleeper, he was homeless. He acted like it. He felt like it. He was it.

So he sat there in the darkness, an occasional car passing anonymously.

He had no idea how long passed before a thought crossed his mind. Ruskin. Or rather, the quote from Ruskin: *The work of science is to substitute facts for appearances and demonstrations for impressions.*

He had no idea why, of all things, his brain had coughed up that. So he just sat there. Not even waiting. Just sitting.

Slowly, something started to buzz in his brain. Like the whine of a mosquito in the night. He let it. He didn't have the energy to care about mosquitoes anymore, even invisible ones inside his own brain.

It whined on. It grew louder. It became a loud noise. Then a scream. Finally, he paid attention to it.

It was Ruskin. Again.

His brain ran through the quote over and over again. Eventually, it stopped on the word "science." *Yes, the scientific method,* he thought. Choose a hypothesis, construct an experiment to test the hypothesis and then analyse the data from the experiment and draw conclusions.

Standing back from what he had done, he could see that choosing a hypothesis was almost impossible without ego, the ego that comes with experience and a professional qualification.

Lose the ego, he told himself.

What other type of science do you know?

Data Science.

Really, when he took a step back and didn't think about it but kind of squinted at it sideways, really then it looked different. The mystery in the file was really nothing more than an open-ended data-science problem. What he really had was many types of data, but no idea what variables might be related to other variables. Or in what way.

Luke turned himself to confront it face on, no longer squinting at it sideways but giving it a good stare instead. And then he winced and looked away from it altogether, looked into the night.

You moron, he thought. *You stupid, egotistical moron.*

He fed that into the black hole of self-loathing that was sucking his lifeforce from him.

He hadn't needed to be clever. He hadn't needed to dream up one hypothesis after another. He just needed to use the right tools and let the data speak.

— . —

Amber paused at the Underground entrance and waved goodbye to her lover. She'd promised Drinkwater she'd go straight home right away, which meant a couple of stops on the Tube. Their quickie had been almost violent, up against a wall in a darkened alley. She wasn't quite sure what to make of it. Had it been good? *Well, kind of,* she qualified, *yes, in a way.* Unexpected. Unasked for. And ... uncomfortable.

She wasn't sure how she felt about it. But now the press of people on the platform felt more oppressive than ever. She didn't like the jostling, the touch of them. Not at the moment. But it wasn't just the closeness of the people, it felt like their eyes were on her. As though somehow, they'd seen what happened in the alley. The train pulled in and it was jammed full of revellers. Amber sighed to herself and thought about sticking out her elbows to get in the carriage.

She'd go straight home. Just on the next train. In five minutes. Which made no difference one way or another. But when it came, she let it too pass.

Then she decided against the Tube completely. She'd walk.

— · —

Manny was waiting at her flat. And waiting. *Fuck this case,* he thought. He was working far too hard for his money. When this bird showed up, he'd make her pay for all this waiting. He was owed it.

— · —

Data science, Luke whispered to himself. Was the computer code from the course he had taken years before still lurking in some dark corner of his laptop? His fingers moved frantically to find it.

The code would allow him to search for correlations between each pair of the many fields in the data file. There might be some important relationships other than those that were expected, and those that could not be detected by the naked human eye. There was no ego in the code.

The methods were at the foundation of what would become Predictive Analytics, and subsequently Artificial Intelligence. Even if he somehow had been able to access his AI accounts, these earlier tools were what he needed for this. Commercial AI packages wrapped everything up in a bow in a split second but didn't tell you how it found the answer. He needed to see under the hood. He needed the answer, but he needed the "how" as well.

There it was! Tucked away. Like all the things that had been tucked away in his backpack.

Problem number one was that his programming skills in Python, the language used for such things, was rusty.

Problem number two was he would need a huge amount of power to do such a run. What would have been considered brute-force computing back in his days of programming was now the norm. However, brute force worked best with cloud computing. It did not work so well for a punter on a bench doing stare-at-a-cloud computing.

But what were his options?

He made what seemed like logical changes, double-checked them, closed his eyes, said a short coder's prayer and ran the programme.

— · —

It was surprisingly quiet as she waited patiently for the red light to turn to green. She still felt knowing eyes on her, like a gentle pressure pressing her on the spot on her back which the brick had rubbed raw.

With the exception of a woman in a burqa sitting on the bench opposite, she could nip across without anyone even noticing. Like a Londoner. Just as she placed her foot in the gutter, a motorcycle skidded around the corner. Amber jumped back. Then a car.

Right, thought Amber, *got it. Be a good girl.* She could hear her parents' voices in her head, exhorting her. The light still wasn't turning green. Amber looked around and saw that she needed to press the pedestrian walk button. She rolled her eyes. And pressed it.

Her curiosity about BMI's mortality data and the whole Luke Smith thing had got her into BMI's executive floor and would ultimately get her a better paying position there. Her father had been right about curiosity. It would be the making of her. Odd though, that Alaistair no longer wanted to discuss it.

— · —

The results had not computed. He'd made a mistake somewhere with his coding changes. His battery had sunk to 10%. The clock ticked towards a new day and a new form of failure.

At least I'm consistent, he'd thought to himself.

But I'm still in the game.

— · —

As she crossed the street, Amber noticed that the woman in the burka was hunkered over a laptop, tapping away. It was a strange time of night for anyone to be checking their email. On the other hand, she might have a small flat with the footie playing loudly, and was probably looking for some peace and quiet. And goodness knows the street was quiet enough. Amber felt a surge of sympathy. She too lived in a place far too cheap and noisy for her tastes – and that's saying something coming from Hong Kong.

As she passed the woman on the bench, Amber's eyes strayed down to the screen and then widened in surprise. There was an awful lot of code being written there. *Well,* Amber thought, *that's taught you not to judge a book by its cover. She's not emailing anyone, she's writing computer code.*

She heard a slight cough behind her. And a voice so quiet Amber had to take a few steps back to hear.

"Power bank? Buy?" It was a raspy whisper.

"A battery?" Amber turned and asked. "For your computer?"

Amber could tell the woman in the burqa was nodding. Amber dug in her leather satchel that she took to work, fishing around for her portable power bank. She'd taken to carrying one on the assumption that she'd be unexpectedly spending time with Alaistair Drinkwater and she didn't want to run out of power on her laptop when she was showing him her latest calculations. As it turned out, he was more interested in other things.

"Here," she said. The lady started to fumble around and pulled out some money. "No, no," she said, shaking her hands back and forth. It would be far easier for her to wait a minute or two than to have to replace the power bank. Amber's eyes widened as the woman pounced on the power bank battery pack and plugged her own computer in with lightning speed.

Amber's eyes naturally went to the computer screen. Then studied it harder. She recognised the Python code.

— · —

He couldn't see her well, not with the shadows and the screen over his eyes, but he could discern a trim feminine figure. As a man, he never would have stopped her. She was a step or two past before the penny dropped: he was no longer the male of the species. He'd breathed out his question. And then had to repeat it. And then almost fumbled the battery pack when it was handed over. He watched as his laptop sucked up the power from her battery pack. It hit 20% before he started to pay attention to the young woman beside him. He couldn't see her very well, even when he swivelled his head.

But by the time the laptop hit 30%, Luke knew that she was eyeballing the stats with an accomplished eye. He just didn't know what do about it.

— · —

"Looks like you're trying to use predictive analysis on this data set," Amber said calmly. "I'm studying this right now, and I have a study group on it tomorrow. It's a struggle, isn't it?" To be an immigrant without family or friends to lean on. And then to spend your Saturdays learning this. She knew what it was like. Until you're far from home and on your own and everyone expects more out of you than you knew how to give, you just can't imagine what it takes to merely get through the day.

Amber realised the lady probably couldn't understand her

English. She dug back into her work bag and plucked out her textbook. "I've been using this. It's the latest edition. It might..." her voice trailed off as the lady snatched the text book and flipped to the table of contents, then to a section, then to a page. Amber recognised the page. The lady's finger traced some code, and then let the book close. She opened the laptop and started typing the code she had just traced. Amber opened the book to the page and held it open next to the laptop. The burqa lady gave Amber a thumbs up.

Amber looked at the clock on her phone. It had been a while since she left Drinkwater. She didn't dare phone him to explain why she wasn't in her flat now. She did notice that he hadn't tried to phone or text her to make sure she'd made it. After all that song-and-dance routine about being safe. She shrugged. She could wonder about that later.

Amber's eyes went back to the coding the lady was doing. She noticed a typo. Just one character, but enough to mess everything up. She pointed at it and the lady stopped typing, went back and fixed the typo. She heard a snort of amusement. Amber smiled. *No need for two coders to struggle in English*, she thought.

Bizarrely she felt she had more in common with this Muslim immigrant lady than with Alaistair Drinkwater with his smooth charm and pointed questions and strange sexual tastes. They waited as the next set of data got crunched. The burqa lady was reading her textbook, or given the way that she was flipping through the pages, reminding herself of how to do things.

The battery clicked up to over 40%. She'd wait until it hit 50%. It wouldn't take long, and it would certainly help this lady out.

Finally, Amber made a regretful face and jerked her thumb to show she needed to go. The lady seemed happy enough to hand over her battery pack. And then she put her hands together in prayer and bent her head over her hands. The universal symbol of gratitude and thanks. Amber did the same in reply.

— · —

Within the block, Amber could hear steps behind her. *Probably just some stumbling late-Friday drunk,* she assumed. But the steps were quicker than hers and coming right towards her. Before she could turn, she felt a hand on the back of her shoulder, pushing her.

Another shove was delivered. Amber took a half step to balance herself and swung around. There was no doubt this was intentional.

"Hey!" she said as she made eye contact with the tall lady with wild eyes.

They stood very close to one another, rage emanating from the tall lady.

"Did you ever fucking think he might be married?" she yelled, some spittle landing on Amber's cheek. "Did you ever think of that?"

Amber connected the dots quickly. "He seems to have needs that are not being met." She tried to increase the space between them.

The woman squinted and her nostrils widened for a moment before she lunged right into Amber's face. "You slut!"

Amber pushed her away, turned and ran. She had the rugby ball now, there was no one between her and touch line, all she had to do was run.

As they ran, the woman yelled, "I can track him, you know."

Amber could tell she was building a lead.

"He doesn't know it, but I have a tracker on his phone," the tall lady shouted. Amber's lead was still increasing. She could lose this bitch pretty quickly.

"You can run, slut, but I know where you live."

Amber rounded a corner and ducked into an alcove as she considered this threat. The lady ran past. She gave it a few seconds and took off in the opposite direction at a sprint. She had

a couple of friends in tomorrow's study group she could probably crash with. Claim to have some sort of landlord issue or
something.

CHAPTER 9:
Saturday

Luke's eyes flickered but he saw nothing but black.

He squinted and opened his eyes again. He was looking straight up among buildings, and could see there was a tiny bit of light in one corner of the sky. He was lying on his back, arms wrapped around the laptop, backpack under his head.

He sat up slowly and painfully, still on the bench he'd been on last night, and opened the laptop.

Totally dead – as expected, he realised groggily. One of the spare batteries he had in his backpack had a little bit of juice left in it, and he swapped that one in. The laptop came back to life.

Bad news was it had died about 10% of the way through the file.

He opened the summary of the analysis it had been able to perform. It listed a perfect correlation between the beneficiary field and the various blood fields, such as blood type. Very strange. And only within a certain section of the file. He scrolled to that section.

The entire screen showed records that had identical values in the beneficiary field. *Was it possible that there were a very large number of policies on one person for some reason?*

The beneficiary for each policy wasn't even a person's name or a person's estate, it was a Cayman's Island SPV, identified by #866426C. He scrolled to the right to look further into the records. While the beneficiary field was exactly the same in all the policies, the insured persons and the dates of death were all different. But even though the names were all different, the blood characteristics of each insured person was recorded as being exactly the same!

And the insured amounts were not small, they were all between one million and five million pounds!

His brow tightened as his mind found a new gear. He knew that Cayman Island SPV stood for Special Purpose Vehicle. While SPVs could be used for legitimate financial structuring, they were also a tool for financial shenanigans. In this case, SPV may as well have stood for *Smoking Pistol Verified*.

The insured were all men. For a few, the cause of death was listed as AIDS. For most of the others, various types of infections that AIDS patients often die from, given their weakened or non-existent immune systems, were listed. Some were non-Hodgkin's lymphoma, some were pneumonia. Luke suspected some doctors might be hesitant to put AIDS on a death certificate. There were no accidental deaths, and only one or two heart attacks.

At that moment, the clouds suddenly parted, and the rising sun suddenly shone through. Luke had it now. He had the breakthrough! The hockey player in him shouted aloud, "He shoots, he scores!" And he instinctively raised his arms in jubilation.

Someone at BMI had access to the identities of AIDS sufferers. A policy would be entered into BMI's administrative systems so that when these people prematurely passed away, the death benefit would flow out of BMI and into the Cayman Islands account. The details required to set up a policy in the system, such as blood data, were cut and pasted into the file to make it appear that these people had been underwritten in the normal fashion. These people, or their estates, wouldn't even know that they had been "insured" in BMI's system. They may even had had other life insurance policies with other companies. But BMI also had a real policy for a real person with a real disease who really died. And it made real money that got deposited in a real account.

It was an ingenious way to get hundreds of millions out of BMI and into this dodgy offshore account.

This could only have been done at the highest level. Braun was all over this one as if he'd autographed each and every entry. He didn't know how many other people knew. Was the new CEO Alaistair Drinkwater in on it? There wasn't a lot of point of stealing millions if you had to share it widely and a CEO is expensive to buy. Luke bet that the only person in on the scam was Braun himself. In another few years he could retire to the Cayman Islands on his legit stock options and savings, but also access this fund if he ever felt skint.

Luke sat without moving for a minute, marvelling at the sheer volume of money stolen.

Very softly, he murmured, "The work of science." The new science was to substitute data for egotism. It had made short work of the problem.

He had a new quandary. He had discovered what he had desperately sought, but only now realised that he had a new challenge in front of him.

How to publicise what he'd found?

If he simply walked into a police station, he would be arrested immediately. Eventually, he might get to air his findings, but only after a protracted trial that would gobble up a significant portion of his remaining lifetime and all his savings. Simply publishing the data on the internet was so legally wrong, NDA or no NDA, that he would be convicted and further vilified, if that were possible, regardless of how shocking his findings were.

— · —

Zofia's eyes widened when she saw the email. She knew who the sender was. This individual was buried deep within the Met's IT security group. Rumour had it that he had worked the graveyard shift every day for decades and never spoke more than one sentence at a time. She felt queasy but started dialling anyway.

"We never had this conversation," she heard without even a hello.

"Okay," she agreed. "Let's have this conversation that we will never have had."

"As you may or may not know, the Met has unofficial access to a number of data sources which cannot be revealed." He paused. She didn't know what to say.

"Let's just say that data has matched your suspect, Mr Smith, with the appearance and movement of an individual who was recorded at the ..." He paused and started doing a very poor job of reading something that was clearly in Polish.

"Yes, that's the Art Gallery at the Polish Centre in Hammersmith." She put him out of his misery as her awakening mind tried to go from zero to sixty. "When did this take place?" She asked.

"Middle of the day on Thursday."

"How can I see this recording?"

"Obviously you don't understand the nature of this call. Which did not take place." The call ended.

She rubbed her forehead. *Was she even awake yet?*

"Who was that?" Petr asked with a furrowed brow. "Do I want to know?"

She thought it through. "You and I need to drive to the Polish Centre this morning when it opens. Even if I'm still puking, you need to get us there."

"On police business?"

"No. Just two Polish people going to the Polish Centre on a Saturday morning."

He didn't move. The furrow in his brow deepened.

"Cmon, get your shit together," she said, a smile creeping onto her lips.

"Yes, officer. I mean, yes ma'am." He corrected himself and returned the smile.

"I thought we were going with Goddess now."

— . —

Alaistair Drinkwater gently massaged the muscle in his cheek, just above his jaw. It ached. Manny was supposed to have phoned when the job was done but he hadn't. Drinkwater was getting seriously hacked off at how much time he spent waiting for Manny to call him.

He couldn't really phone Amber. The police would find a record of the call and he'd be interviewed. And that added a complication he didn't need.

But if Manny hadn't phoned that meant she had slipped through the net. Again. He ground his teeth, ignoring the shot of pain up the side of his face and into his hairline.

Fuck this, he thought savagely. *I'm going to have to do it.*

— . —

King Street was completely empty and lifeless at that early hour of the morning. Luke caught sight of himself in a large picture window he was passing. He stopped and marvelled at how well the burka worked. The black head-cover had a slit for sight and sat on his nose effectively. The tunnel vision effect of looking through the slit was exactly what he expected. He resisted the urge to swing his head around constantly to have a wider range of sight. The outfit hung on his shoulders and went to within a couple of inches of the ground.

He felt amazing. He whistled Streets of London to himself, an ode to the homeless, and somehow it felt jaunty. He felt jaunty. He swung his arms as if to skip. And caught another glimpse of himself in a window.

He ground to a halt, barely able to stop himself from laughing aloud. He didn't look like a devout Muslim housewife out doing her morning shopping. He looked like … a well-lubricated bloke going home from a dress-up party.

Stop celebrating, he told himself sharply. *It's not over yet. You've got to get this information out now.*

But the euphoria was overriding his fear. And he started to sing the song quietly to himself as he walked the streets of London. *Have you seen the old man reading yesterday's news?*

And suddenly Luke knew what he had to do.

— · —

Cracking his eyes open, Manny glanced at his alarm clock. It was 7:30, a full two hours later than he normally got up to work out. Even this degree of movement reminded him how hard he'd fallen off the wagon last night. He'd waited for the Asian babe to show up and once again, she hadn't appeared. After midnight, he popped into his local for last call. And then, out of frustration, he had gone to an off-licence for more. Killing was frustrating. Or least, trying to kill this one was.

He slid his fingers over his phones to make sure he hadn't missed anything. He bolted straight up when he saw that he had a voice message from Jocko.

"Hey Sarge. This is Jocko. Can you hear this?" Jocko's voice came through. "We found the Smith guy last night. He stepped into a bar on King Street in Hammersmith with a turban on. Our guys asked to see his ear and he took off. We chased him but he was too fast for us. He went to the Hammersmith Bridge. We thought he went over, but we didn't find him there. Cops appeared because people said that someone jumped in the river. We thought it might be him, but we didn't say anything to anyone."

Manny's head hurt. *That police shit going on by the river last night, could that have been Smith? I had been so close – if only I hadn't been drinking.*

Manny phoned Jocko back and Jocko fumbled an answer in surprise. After a few pleasantries, Manny got granular about what happened. Jocko was forthcoming about everything except the last meeting. Manny then wrapped it up.

"Thanks, Sarge," Manny said. "I'll take it from here. And when I catch this fucker, I'll be splitting the earnings with you 50-50. I can almost feel the cash in our hands." And he hung up before listening to Jocko's reply.

The good news was that the trail of the crook with the cauliflower ear, having been dormant for many days, was hot. That meant he needed to move.

Manny checked the tides and knew the water had been high last night. If Smith had chosen to fight the tide, there was really nowhere for him to get out of the water. So he would have gone with the tide. He scanned the map for places that he could have hauled himself out. These were the logical starting points for today's search.

Within a minute of arriving back at Furnivall Gardens, Manny found the campsite again. And this time he ripped it apart. Literally. As he surveyed the nearby underbrush, he saw the corner of a piece of luggage. *A treasure trove no doubt,* he thought, as he pulled the luggage out of the dirt and branches, and then noticed a large backpack hidden close by as well. He could have predicted what would be in there: the jetboil, a gas canister for it, some food, some average-sized men's clothes. In the bottom of the luggage there was some sort of flyer.

It was not in English, and Manny was momentarily disappointed as it implied that the camper had not been Smith. The word *biblioteka* caught his eye, and he remembered the word for library in French was *biblioteque*. He pictured Smith, in a turban, sitting in a library. A library would probably be a great place to do computer work.

Manny gave a private smile, the kind he kept for himself and his football team when it unexpectedly performed. He was now hot on Smith's trail. On the flyer, he saw the address on King Street. But first, he needed to get there. He texted Simon.

— · —

Petr felt nervous as he and Zofia walked up to the Polish Centre. He didn't understand what was going on, but this was the first time that he'd had any involvement at all in what she did. She stopped beside the beggar, who was, as usual, close to the door, and dropped a twenty in his jar.

"I'm looking for a man who wears a black turban and I'm told is in this area often. Do you know him?" Her voice was casual, as if the homeless man was known to her.

The guy deliberately looked her up and down and was quiet for a minute until he responded, "I don't know what you are talking about."

She looked him in the eye for a couple of seconds, nodded in thanks and then proceeded through the door.

Very strange, Petr thought.

They went across the lobby straight to the entrance to the art gallery, only to discover that it wasn't yet open. But he wasn't even sure what they would have done if it was. It's not like Smith would be curled up in the corner or anything. A number of people said a passing hello to the pair of them, and as he had expected, it wasn't more than two minutes before he was in a conversation with a former worker.

He positioned himself to keep half an eye on Zofia. Under the circumstances, she couldn't start asking specific questions, and he could see that she was getting frustrated.

"I'm going to the office," she eventually said.

"On a Saturday?" he asked, before wondering why he had responded that way.

"There's nothing to do here. I'm not sure what I was thinking." Zofia was frustrated. Her kidnap theory was clearly wrong since he was hanging out here at the Polish Centre. There was no secret shagging with Vicky Headley as he hadn't scarpered with the data. He had been here the whole time, with his laptop and data file. But why? It wasn't as if he needed any help to figure it out. Data was his nine to five. He could do this stuff in his sleep. "I'll go to IT and see if I can make some progress that way. Why don't you stay here and hang with your friends?"

She turned and walked away. He stared at her as he always did when he got a chance. He could tell that she felt foolish and wished there was something that he could do to help.

— · —

Luke's trip to the post office went as planned with one small hiccup. When he reached for the roll of banknotes in his pocket, he had to reach under the burqa to do so. Instead of putting the notes back in his pocket, he put it in his backpack to avoid that awkwardness in the future.

He then walked straight to the Tekno Bar. As he went to open the door, he saw that there was a queue at the cash register. He closed the door and kept going to the Medjool Market. He would come back in a few minutes.

He needed things he could eat easily that day, without cooking. He chose some dates from the display outside. He was reaching for a banana when his arm brushed against another shopper reaching for the same banana. He held onto the banana and the other person let go.

"Sorry ma'am," Manny said as he let go of the banana.

Manny went inside the store to pay for his banana and red grapes. Luke was not far behind. He grabbed a newspaper off the top of the pile on his way through the door. Luke then went to the back of the store to grab a drink, a bag of salted cashews and a bag of almonds. He stood right behind Manny as Manny paid.

They exited the Medjool Market three feet apart, Manny in front. Manny was making a beeline for the Polish Centre, Luke for the Tekno Bar. Within the first few steps, Luke realised that he had a problem. *How does one eat or drink while wearing such a head covering?* He made a quick left towards Ravenscourt to figure this out.

— · —

Manny didn't know what to expect when he entered the Polish Centre. There were people coming and going as well as lots of signs, posters and other information in the lobby. Eventually, he saw the sign for the library, opened the door and headed up the stairs.

The library was completely quiet. He saw the desktop computers at the end of the room, and he could picture Smith sitting there. He checked the bathroom but there wasn't a soul in it so he went back to the front desk.

Petr was standing close to the reception desk, looking at his phone and texting two of his workers. Both his construction sites were active that day and he was trying to determine which one to go to first.

"Maybe you can help me?" Manny asked the lady at reception. "I'm looking for a man who wears a black turban. His mother is my neighbour and she is very sick. She mentioned that he spends time here."

Petr overheard the unusual conversation and his attention left his text messages.

"Oh yes," the lady said right away. "He here at library every day for week. Only goes to library." She stood up and pointed to the door to the library. "Work on computers up there."

Manny nodded. He was so astonished that he had found Smith's trail that he didn't know what question to ask next.

"Thanks again. Very nice facility you have here," he said, moving his head to each side and looking around the entire lobby.

The lady smiled and turned her head down to her reading.

Manny sat down on one of the benches. *What next?* he wondered. Smith was not coming here to study Polish but to do something with this data file. *But he wasn't here now. So where could he be?*

The cogs were turning quickly in Petr's head. *Why were Zofia and this guy asking the same question? Why would a man in a turban be in the Polish Centre? Unless ... he really needed to use a computer, and the turban is supposed to hide something ... like a disfigured ear! This guy right here must be a Smith-hunter! And he's onto something! Zofia had said a number of times that a private citizen would probably find Smith before the Met did.*

Manny left the library. Petr followed.

— · —

Luke ate the banana and some of the dates in Ravenscourt. He also finished about half of the deliciously cold and caffeinated iced tea he'd bought. He did this by finding a bench that was a little out of the way, and simply lifting the head covering enough to eat and to drink.

As he walked past the Polish Centre, Link's eyes followed him.

When he got to the Tekno Bar, there was only one person waiting at the cash register. Luke took off his backpack and took out his laptop. When he got to the front of the line, he held up the laptop and said slowly, "Flash drive," while holding up three fingers.

"3MG?" The young man asked.

Luke shook his head.

"Three flash drives?" the young man asked, slightly surprised.

Luke nodded. "Battery," he breathed. The young man nodded casually and went to the storeroom.

After that, it was a quick and easy transaction. Luke was thankful he had his money handy in his backpack, and not in his trouser pocket. There were a few high-top tables at the front of the store. He sat down at the empty one.

At the post office, he bought some envelopes and paper. Then he wrote three copies of a note, one for each envelope. He pulled out the newspaper he'd bought at the Medjool Market, found the address he needed and printed it on one of the envelopes. He was certain he knew enough of the address for the second and third envelopes. He put on the required postage on each of them.

He created a new small file that contained the condemning records and put notes in the file detailing what he'd discovered, and the Python code he had used. The laptop was now busy copying the small file over to one of the flash drives he had bought. It was taking forever. *This is the cyber version of waiting for water to boil,* he thought. *Except it takes far longer.*

He was nervous. His new disguise was working, but he was within a few hundred yards of where he had been discovered the night before. He could almost see the pub from where he was sitting. He was anxious to keep moving.

Manny left the Polish Centre and was walking east down King Street, trying to determine where Smith might be, or where else Smith might have spent time. As he walked past the Tekno Bar, he saw that there were people sitting at the small high-top tables in the front, staring at the devices in front of them. As he processed this, he stopped and entered the store.

Manny's sudden move caught Petr by surprise, and the two collided. When Manny went in the store, Petr waited on the pavement, pretending to look at his phone.

The two pedestrians bumping like a '70s disco caught Luke's attention. He watched the man open the door and, as he walked in, he was five yards away from Luke and facing him directly.

It was the guy with the gun!

— · —

Amber settled down to do her practice test. Despite the sheer volume of coffee that she'd tossed down her throat, she was still groggy from her lack of sleep. It wasn't just the too-few hours studying the insides of her lids, it was that every time she closed her eyes, Alaistair Drinkwater was there, his wife by his side. The couch hadn't been the best either.

The instructor slipped out of the room, probably to have a cigarette. The other students, each as diligent as the next, were hyper-focused with their heads down.

As was Amber. Usually.

— · —

Zofia felt her phone vibrate as traffic moved ahead. She assumed it was Petr. The call ended as she came to a stop. It was Maria and the text "URGENT CALL ME ASAP" came up immediately. As Zofia thumbed the number and the call icon, she kept an eye on the red light. Maria could barely speak she was so excited.

"Big break in your case. Maybe you saw that the murder victim they found in the Thames was finally identified."

Zofia almost gasped.

"They just let one of our new AI tools loose on her and it had a field day in a split second. She's an actuary, works at Silverthorne Staley, the investment bank working on the British Mutual Insurance IPO."

Zofia's heart jumped.

"She wasn't working on the deal though."

Zofia's heart sank.

"But her last communication was to another young female actuary who was on the same deal team as Luke Smith, so also a consultant. Name is Amber Leung. Apparently Amber Leung and the victim were friends. The machine even said they looked similar. Sending you Leung's number now."

"Holyyy shiitt!" Her heart ricocheted from sinking to racing.

The cars behind Zofia honked. She tried to focus simultaneously on the traffic and the news. Couldn't. Pulled over in a bus lay-by. She took a deep breath. She dialled Leung's number.

— · —

The man was dressed the same way, moved the same way. There was no doubt in Luke's mind that it was the guy from the Bureau de Change back on Bayswater Road. The man walked right past Luke's table and stood in the line by the cashier ten feet away. Luke closed his laptop, stuck it in his backpack and exited the store as quickly as he could without attracting notice. He needed to go downtown – *immediately*!

He saw a minicab stopped at the end of Cromwell Road. He ran towards it without thinking how this might look.

"Friday Street?" he asked loudly as he approached the driver.

Simon looked up slowly but didn't respond.

"In the City," Luke snapped, before wondering why he had opened his mouth again.

"Sorry, I'm booked, lady," Simon responded, as he looked back down at the racing form page.

Luke turned back to King Street. He was scanning the area for the man with the gun but trying not to swing his head around too obtrusively. The limited range of vision allowed by the burqa was now a real problem. He felt very vulnerable standing still on the curb of the street.

Suddenly, the screech of a cab's brakes and a woman's high-pitch yelp of astonishment turned all the heads on the street, including Luke's.

On the opposite side of the street, Link stood in the middle of the road facing a taxi with an enraged driver. Link turned to Luke and motioned him into the taxi. Luke dashed across the street and flung himself into the cab as Link stepped back to the pavement.

"Friday Street, please," he said in a slow indistinct monotone.

"As you wish." Then the driver added a sarcastic "luv" as he drove away.

— · —

"Hello."

"Hello Amber, this is Constable Zofia Dabrowski from the Metropolitan Police Force."

Silence.

"Is this Amber Leung?"

"Yes, it is," Amber replied meekly.

"I've just texted my name to you. If you'd like to, call the number for the Met and ask to be put through to me."

"Just go ahead." Would she have to leave the country for some reason? Was it her visa? She'd read that when the Home Office rejected you, you had twenty-four hours to leave the country. What would her boss say? And her parents? How would she ever overcome the shame?

"I have some very serious news. I'm sorry to say that Xiaowei Deng was found murdered on Wednesday late evening."

Zofia waited. There was silence. Eventually, she said, "I know this is very difficult, but we need to take action right away. Hello? Can I keep going?"

"Yes," came back quietly as Amber began to consider the life of guilt and shame that lay ahead of her.

"Her last communication was a text sent to you late Wednesday night. Near as we can determine, you were the last person she contacted."

A terrible grief rose in Amber. Like a wodge of pain, it blocked her from speaking.

"Are you there, Ms Leung?"

After a long silence, Amber began to speak. "Yes, she and I were supposed to be at a networking dinner together. I invited her but I stood her up."

Zofia was encouraged to hear Amber finally speak. "How unfortunate," she murmured. And she meant it. "It seems you were part of the team that Luke Smith was part of."

"I was."

"We haven't put all the pieces together, but I'm concerned your life is in danger." She wanted all of this to go much quicker and didn't wait for a response. "Where are you now?"

"City of London Boys School, beside St Paul's Cathedral in the City. I'm taking an actuarial class."

Zofia let Amber rattle off the information. It was nerves. "Stay where you are until we meet you there. We will show our credentials. Please don't do anything until we get there. I will call you back in one minute and we will leave that call open so we can find you quickly. Understood, Amber?"

"Yes, I hear you."

"Great." Zofia hung up.

— . —

When he entered the Tekno Bar, Manny asked a similar question to the one he had asked a number of times that day about a man in a black turban looking for computer supplies.

"Don't recall a black turban," the scruffy young man answered. "There's a large Middle Eastern community round here … why just a few minutes ago a lady in one of those head coverings bought a huge amount of storage … we don't see the face veils in here too often. I've no idea how they can see anything."

"Thanks," Manny said as he stepped out of line. He squinted as things fell in place inside his head and created electricity in the process. If Smith had computer work to do that involved a lot of data and he was trying to hide his ear after he had been discovered in his turban, then …

"What a sly bugger I'm chasing!" he said softly to himself as he burst out of the store onto the high street. He went to the curb and looked up and down the street but he couldn't see the black burqa. Swearing, he ran to the minicab.

When Petr saw the man burst out of the store, he went to camera mode on his phone as fast as he could. He got a couple of pictures of the back of the running man, even though he knew they would be useless pictures. The man stopped at a taxi and spoke to the driver. Petr zoomed and clicked.

"The bastard's wearing a face veil now," Manny blurted to Simon. "He was just in that computer store. Can't be far. Did you see him?"

"There was a tall lady wearing one of those things who just asked me to give her a ride to Friday Street. She had her knickers in a real twist. She hopped into a cab on the high street right after that."

"That was him! Start the car! Get us to Friday Street before he gets there!" Manny yelled.

They both knew what was on Friday Street. And Manny knew exactly why Smith was headed there.

— · —

When Petr saw the man get in the minicab, he stuck his hand in the air immediately. Within seconds he heard the screeching of a taxi stopping and he hopped in.

"Follow that cab!" he commanded, pointing to it a few vehicles in front.

— · —

Zofia called in as soon as she hung up.

"This is Constable Zofia Dabrowski. I need armed backup at the City of London School. I will be there in ... three minutes."

"Okay Constable. Your armed backup is on its way."

Zofia could hear rapid keystrokes in the background. "What is your situation?"

"Protecting a witness in danger. I need to stay in contact with the witness." She ended the call.

"Armed backup!" The dispatcher said quietly to himself. He could see Dabrowski's profile. She was a rookie. A raw rookie at that.

In thirty years on the force, he had never heard of a rookie constable calling for armed backup. He rolled his eyes. Armed backup! She's played one too many video games. Plus – and this was not a detail – he had never been hung up on by a constable before. He looked at her chain of command and slowly smiled. She'd get her wrists slapped for this one. This would end up as a learning experience for a rookie. But his arse was covered.

— · —

After a short distance, Luke pulled out his laptop. The file had copied onto the first flash drive. He took the flash drive out and put it in one of the envelopes. He put the second flash drive into the laptop and started the copying process again.

— · —

The signs for the actuarial class took him to a large classroom on the ground floor. As he casually peered in the door at the rear of the classroom, he could see the backs of the heads of the students, five of whom were Asian women. Everyone in the room had their heads down, focused on a screen or a book or their notes. He wasn't entirely sure which one was Amber and didn't want to bring any attention to himself. He slipped inside and waited.

He heard the soft buzz of a phone and one of them put her phone to her ear and got up to take the call. He caught a glimpse of who it was. And smiled like a coyote. Then he hunkered over his desk, trying not to be seen.

But she sat back down almost immediately. The blood drained from her face before her hand came up in front of her mouth. It looked like she might even fall off the chair and onto the floor. It was clear she was receiving some very bad news.

He slipped from his seat and moved closer. She looked up, terrified. Then her face softened. "Alaistair," she began, her eyes filling with tears.

He nodded his head to the back. "C'mon," he mouthed at her.

She was completely frozen. "Why are you here? I have class."

He jerked his head to the back again and smiled winningly. She dropped her head into her hands, rocking slightly.

He leaned over and breathed gently on her cheek. "Tell me about it outside." He was desperate to leave before these boffins lifted their heads from their work and could identify him.

Still she sat there. He suppressed his impatience but laid a hand under her elbow and pushed firmly up.

Moving at a glacier pace, she stood. He gently steered her towards the back entrance of the classroom where they were unlikely to be seen. She moved like a dead weight, pausing on each step as if just lifting her foot exhausted her. He kept a gentle but firm forward pressure as she all but stopped.

As soon as she got into the hallway, she did stop.

The grinding of his teeth was audible.

"I have to stay here," she told him flatly. "Someone is meeting me."

A spasm of rage so profound it mutated into hate slid across his face. He crowded her against the wall, caging her with his much larger body. His arm dived into his jacket and pulled out a knife. It was a killing instrument, finely honed and double-edged, slim and deadly.

"You're too clever for your own good," he hissed. And raised the knife to strike.

— · —

Luke was fighting the constant urge to look over his shoulder every second since he had spotted the gunman. Instead, his sole focus was on copying the flash drives. Eventually, the file finished copying to the second flash drive so he put it into the second envelope, and started the copying process for the third flash drive.

He turned far enough towards the window to recognise that they were approaching the central financial district of the City. His anxiety to get the envelopes on their way and to get himself to his destination, was mounting.

As they pulled up to a red stoplight, Luke noticed the outline of St. Paul's Cathedral and knew they were close to Friday Street. He could see a post box on the pavement a few yards away from where they were stopped. He said, "This is fine," to the cabbie and started handing him bills. In a few seconds, he was out of the cab.

Luke quickly put the two sealed envelopes into the post box.

One envelope was addressed to *The London Standard*. He had taken the address from the newspaper he'd bought that morning at the Medjool Market. The other envelope was to the *Prudential Regulation Authority*. The PRA was part of the Bank of England, which regulated both banks and insurers in the UK. He knew that in the US there was specific legislation, known as whistleblower protection, for people to come forward when they saw a bank doing something outside of regulations. He didn't know if there was an analogous framework in the UK but if there was, it was probably through the PRA.

He remembered that the Bank of England was on Threadneedle Street. You couldn't forget a name like that. The name was used on occasion in articles describing the Bank of England's actions. He didn't know the street number or postal code, so he had simply written *Prudential Regulation Authority, Bank of England* on the envelope, and *Threadneedle Street* and *London* below that.

He felt very relieved to have made the mailing. The two easiest parts of this three-pronged plan were complete. But he knew deep down that these were longshots. How many institutions answered snail mail from random people?

Probably none.

The third flash drive hadn't finished copying yet. But the most important thing now was to get to the finish line, whether he had a copied flash drive or not. He wanted to turn himself in in his own way, and do all of this before the guy with the gun, or anyone else, stopped him.

He put the backpack on and walked towards Friday Street. As he walked, he had to navigate around St. Paul's Cathedral. He marvelled at such a landmark sitting among modern office buildings. He knew it would feel like a sanctuary, like he had been transported to a different world, if he went inside.

Stick to the task, he said to himself. *You're so close to the finish line. You don't need sanctuary now. Later, maybe.*

He automatically checked all the church's doors to see which ones were open.

— · —

The kick was fast and powerful. And direct to his balls. Drinkwater leaped backwards, her foot glancing off his upper thigh. But his arm was already in motion. Striking down with all the force he could muster.

But she was also in motion, spinning and running. The knife sliced down the length of her leg, from hip to knee. Her leg exploded in agony. And still she ran.

"Drop your weapon!" Barked from the opposite direction.

Drinkwater whipped around to meet the new threat. The man with the gun was almost on top of him. With a giant leap, Drinkwater managed to get on top of him, his knife falling and stabbing and slicing.

The policeman's gun flew out of his hand across the floor.

Zofia had been behind him, waddling determinedly to keep up. The gun slid right at her feet.

She looked at the man sprinting off. The officer held his shoulder and sank slowly against the wall, the blood welling between his fingers. The knife had got him between the edge of his Kevlar and his arm. He looked at his gun. Then looked at her.

"Chase him," he said softly. "I'll call it in."

A flower of blood blossomed on his shoulder and grew down his arm. She picked up the weapon as she peered around the corner. She saw the man momentarily as he turned the corner of another hallway, and she ran after him as best she could, gun drawn.

— · —

The officer was struggling to reach his radio with his left hand. He saw a large pool of his own blood. He felt things get fuzzy. He used the last of his energy to reach. Then he lost consciousness.

Amber sprinted through the doorway and turned left down a long hall. She had the rugby ball now, the door at the end of the hall was the touch line and no one or nothing was going to catch her.

— · —

Zofia could see her target. He'd exited the school and was moving towards the typical crowd near St Paul's Cathedral. She lost sight of him in the throng but regained it. She could see that he was chasing a young woman, who must be Amber Leung. She was dragging her leg and trailing blood.

Zofia was running with the gun in her hand. There was no holster or anything to put the gun in, which was just as well, she wanted it in her hand.

Her heart was pounding furiously. She had no idea how this was going to end. She only knew that the man with the knife was closing in on Amber, and that she was losing ground on him.

— . —

As Luke rounded the corner onto Friday Street, he saw the man with the gun getting out of a minicab. Although they were fifty yards apart, their eyes met and locked tight, as if they were face to face.

Luke spun and sprinted the other way. He pulled off his head covering just as a car screeched to a halt a few feet from him. A cyclist veered to avoid the car and Luke. Only Luke extended his arm and knocked the cyclist off the bike.

Still at a gallop, Luke hopped on the bike. Bystanders started yelling at Luke when he stole the bike. Standing on the pedals, Luke was riding furiously with Manny only a few yards behind. One man tried to step in front of the bike but thought the better of it as Luke accelerated towards him. Petr ran ten yards behind Manny, holding his phone in front of him. Others ran too. Shouts of "It's him!" "Get him!" "Reward!" could be heard as Saturday's bustle turned to bedlam.

People streamed from stores, jumped out of their cars and abandoned their tourism. What started as greed became its own life force. Those who wanted no part were swept along with little choice as the surge of humanity focused on one objective sucked them all up and turned them into a mob.

As Luke got the bike to a higher speed, he started to pull away from Manny and the other runners. To get back to Friday Street and the Financial Times, Luke made a quick right in front of oncoming cars down a tight alleyway. As the alleyway widened into a proper street, he looked behind to see the gunman still in pursuit, with a growing mob running and yelling behind him.

Manny recognised Luke's strategy of getting back to Friday Street and knew Luke would have to turn right onto Queen

Victoria Street and then quickly right again onto Friday Street. This turn would be Manny's last chance to get him.

Luke jumped the curb and made a blind right turn onto the pavement of Queen Victoria Street.

There was no one in his path. The block was short. He lowered his head for more speed. He simultaneously heard the shot and felt the thud in the middle of his back. The laptop had been hit at just enough of an angle to deflect the bullet and not absorb it.

But the force sent him over the handlebars as the second shot hit the seat of the bike. His left hand hit the pavement first, followed by his left shoulder and his left cheekbone. The force of the second shot vaulted the bike onto Luke's body. Manny lowered his sights to the motionless target.

— · —

Amber staggered into the crowd and let them almost sweep her along, buoyed on each side by the sheer heft of bodies. She reached out and grabbed arms, throwing her weight on their shoulders. She began to see blackness like puddles of spilled espresso. She had no idea where Drinkwater was. She started to fall.

As she sank into the ground, she flung her final thought out to the universe. "I'm sorry. Truly, I tried."

— · —

In the seconds it took Manny to lower his aim for this easy kill, the mob turned blindly onto the street and its momentum sent them crashing into Manny's back. The third shot went high in the air, Manny fell to the ground, his gun bounced on the pavement.

With the sounds of gunshot echoing against the buildings, people screamed and scattered. The crowd behind stumbled back. At his eye level, Manny could see bodies pushing in all directions, feet stomping, the occasional stumble and fall. Manny pushed himself to his feet. He snatched his gun up and raced towards the corner of Friday Street.

He could see Simon's cab waiting for him. He could see Luke scrambling for the Financial Times. He needed to end this. Now.

He took careful aim.

— · —

As she rounded the corner on Friday Street, Zofia couldn't see Amber or the man chasing her. With the sound of the gunshots echoing off the buildings, people were throwing themselves flat or pouring into stores or pressed against walls.

She had a clear view.

A man with a gun taking careful aim.

From his stomach, Petr glimpsed Zofia, the only one on their feet besides the shooter. Another person rolled on top of him in an attempt to get lower. He scrambled up and over the bodies, desperate to get to Zofia, took an elbow in the face and kissed asphalt again. He heard a shot. Then another. There was a heartbeat of silence.

Then he heard sirens.

When Petr was able to look again, he saw the skinny girl from the Polish Centre holding her water bottle out in front of her. She released the water bottle from her outstretched hand, and it became a gun by the time it hit the ground. She staggered forwards and backwards, and then the constable kneeled down slowly, picked up the gun and stood tall, looking down at the fallen, motionless man.

— · —

Luke came storming through the door of the Financial Times building as the third and fourth shots rang out, holding his left arm against his stomach with his right, blood streaming from his face.

He tripped over a person on his way through the security portal and fell, then rolled behind a wall that shielded him from anyone coming through the door. With his face against the marble floor and his knees bent, Luke approached a foetal position.

"Don't move," the guard commanded.

"That man is shooting–"

"Don't move!" The guard yelled again, his voice rising in stress.

Luke lay there, as motionless as humanly possible.

The guard moved his eyes towards the lobby without moving his head or his body. Two minutes later, with no further shots heard, the guard's partner appeared at his side. "I've secured the lobby. We're securing the rest of the ground floor."

"I'm Luke Smith," Luke said, trying to sound calm. It was impossible for the security personnel to not see his ear. "I need to give a flash drive in my backpack to your editor!" He said it loudly, with the bravado of a doomed man. Either this worked or his life as he knew it would be over.

As he spoke, he could taste his own blood. He squeezed his eyes closed as the blood started to seep into his left eye. He was in intense physical pain but could feel finish-line euphoria starting to wash over him at the same time.

— · —

Zofia gasped for air.

The sirens started to penetrate her consciousness. Her first real thought was that she was in plainclothes, pointing a gun. She tried to yell "Police!" but it came out as a whisper.

— · —

Jane, who had been sitting in the corner of the kitchen watching her phone, jumped to her feet. "Ladies! Turn on the telly! RIGHT AWAY!"

Startled, Vicky turned on the BBC.

The video of the pavement of Bread Street froze and zoomed in on a cyclist leading a single chaser, followed by a mob in pursuit. The video ended as the rider and his pursuers turned onto Queen Victoria Street.

The voiceover said, "Ten days ago, Londoners were captivated by the story of the rogue actuary who disappeared with the personal data of thousands of dead people. Today they're spellbound again as he resurfaced in dramatic fashion. The following chase scene isn't a movie. It was recorded by a bystander this afternoon in the vicinity of Bread Street. It shows someone believed to be the actuary, Luke Smith, racing away from a crowd of justice-seeking civilians."

Vicky dropped her head in her hands. "I'm not even sure that's him."

"Who else would it be?" Jane said, putting her arm around Vicky's shoulders and squeezing her.

"But why is everyone chasing him?" Vicky asked.

"Because they want the hundred grand." Jane said. "You're the only one who's crazy about the man and not the money." There was silence as Vicky continued to hold her head in her hands. "Hey, your white knight is coming back to rescue you," Jane said, shaking Vicky slightly, "riding a rental bike. But he's back!"

There was an audible chuckle from behind Vicky's hands and she pulled them away to reveal a face full of tears.

Fiona and Jane's phones buzzed simultaneously. Solemn looks hit their faces as they realised what the type of message would reach both of their phones at the exact same time. They stepped away, stood shoulder-to-shoulder and opened the message. It was the "officer down" message, concluding with, "This is NOT a drill."

The BBC's video suddenly stopped midway and the presenter came back on the screen. "There are now reports from the scene that multiple shots were fired."

While Vicky gasped, the two policewomen were stony-faced. They already knew who was down.

— · —

The veterans were tired and discouraged. They had spent the day searching the entire area in which they had seen Smith the night before. The return to camp was like a death march. That evening, they had asked passers-by if there was anything new on the case and had received sporadic updates that way. They had been so close to catching Smith!

Jocko saw the welcome sight of a lady who regularly provided baked goods to the homeless. A little sugar certainly wouldn't hurt. As she got closer, his heart sank when it was clear there was no pie coming their way. "Me whole family's been huddled 'round our telly with the news so I didn't get to my baking. Whole city is watching this Smith thing and we felt you gents should be too." She handed a phone to Jocko. "It's fully charged and the password's attached. I'll be back early tomorrow to trade you a pie or two for the phone."

Jocko handed the phone to one of the men who propped it up on some boxes, and the campers debated how they should be seated so that the maximum number of them could see and hear the news.

— · —

The bedlam at the scene was still building. More police streamed in, triaging the wounded and pressing people back and away.

Petr had sworn he would not loosen his hold on Zofia until she loosened hers. He could see that the gentleman approaching him directly was the one who had been supervising numerous officers. He broke his promise to himself and let go of Zofia. As soon as his hand was free, it was shaken.

"Chief Inspector Sean McConley."

"Petr Dabrowski. I have video of a lot of it, from the Polish

Centre to here. I can show you the cab that brought the shooter to here and what the shooter did at every step." Zofia kept one arm around Petr but turned to face McConley, while wiping the tears from her eyes.

"Thank you. Hopefully, we'll be able to pick up his accomplices. There will be a medal hanging around your neck very soon, Constable," he announced to Zofia. "I can't tell you how proud I am, and how proud the whole force is of you and your actions today."

A circle had formed around the three of them, and there was applause. Zofia could not wipe away the tears fast enough.

"The officer is in the hospital. He has serious injuries, but they aren't life threatening. I don't believe you are physically injured, but the stretcher behind me is for you, and the ambulance is for the pair of you. I can order you to take it, but I hope I don't have to. You will have the best of care. No one deserves it more."

He inched closer to her, wondering if she would extend her hand, and ended up in a full embrace.

— . —

In the melee, no one noticed a well-dressed man easing his way through the crowd and away from it all. Given the utter chaos, he had hours. If Amber bled out, then he was home free. If she didn't, then it would be her word against his. No one had really seen him, not even the officer he'd knifed. And there was no reason to suspect him. There was nothing to tie him to this. And with his money he could buy himself an alibi.

But he had to go to the dentist. That muscle in his jaw was excruciating.

— . —

News services were trying to piece together all the events. Various videos of the bike chase had been posted online, some showing Smith getting on the rental bike and ripping off the headpiece of the burqa. The news was on a cycle because there was little to add.

— · —

The BBC's flagship news programme interrupted its own broadcast. "We have a statement from Smith himself. We're going live to bring you the news in real time." The reader's voice betrayed his own curiosity.

The video showed Luke seated at a table in a non-descript room. His left arm was in a sling, and the left side of his face was heavily bandaged. There was still some blood caked into the stubble on his chin. It could easily have been a video of a hostage asking for ransom to be paid for their release were it not for his obvious happiness.

"Good afternoon, my name is Luke Smith," he said turning his left ear to the camera for a moment. "I have information about the file of BMI insurance claims that I was given to analyse as part of the IPO preparation." He was calm and spoke confidently, a clear contrast to the newscaster. "The file contains hundreds of claims, totalling hundreds of millions of pounds, which were paid to a Cayman Islands account."

He paused to let the information sink in, the way he'd been taught to give PowerPoint presentations.

"Based on the causes of death of these individuals, it appears that policies were placed on unhealthy people, almost certainly without their knowledge. The eventual death claims from these policies would essentially launder money out of BMI and into the Cayman Islands account. It is impossible for me to know where the money went once it got to the Cayman Islands."

He paused again.

"I'm sure this ordeal has caused a lot of anxiety among a lot of people, including BMI policyholders and the families of the deceased. This is very unfortunate. I have evaded the police over this period of time in order to find the truth, and I will now surrender to the police."

People huddled around TVs in bars and living rooms either lifted their arms or let their shoulders sag. Money changed hands. Attendance at sporting events was down. Many struggled to keep the whole Smith story straight.

— · —

Later in the day, there was a second news event.

"Good afternoon. I am Dieter Braun, Finance Director of BMI. I want to shed light on some of the death claims that BMI has paid." The video showed Braun seated in the BMI boardroom with oil paintings of BMI's past presidents on the wall behind him. His shaved head was reflecting the lights in the ceiling, which none of the PR staff were brave enough to tell him. There was nothing in writing in front of him. He looked straight into the camera.

"British Mutual Insurance has served the British public for over one hundred years." He paused to let everyone absorb that proud history. "Every year AIDS claims thousands of lives. People who are in their prime. People who are smart, hard-working and contributing to society. AIDS has been with us now for more than four decades, claiming over forty million lives.

"Some years ago, BMI's then president and CEO, along with myself and our head of underwriting, decided to do something about the slow progress on HIV and AIDS. All three of us had friends who had died of AIDS.

"The former CEO has since passed away and the former head of underwriting has fallen victim to AIDS himself. Indeed, my best friend from my youth died of AIDS, as have many of our community. I miss them all terribly. My friends were among those I have loved the most in my whole life and it is impossible for me to describe the loss of them. May they rest in peace and still be proud of what we did."

Beads of sweat were now visible on his temples.

"At that time, there was considerable shame in dying of AIDS. Funding to find a treatment was at best insecure. Here at BMI, we had access to the personal details of those who were at risk of AIDS. We used that information to create fake life insurance policies. The people that we 'insured'" – Braun put bunny ears around the word – "knew nothing about this. Nonetheless, their deaths automatically triggered claims to be paid into an offshore account that we set up as the beneficiary. That money was then funnelled into AIDS research. We have funded hundreds of millions of pounds worth of AIDS research this way."

He began to lean closer to the camera, like this was his sales pitch.

"And it worked!" His eyes widened and his nostrils flared. "We have long-acting drugs. We need to make them longer acting. We need them to be low-cost and globally accessible, especially now that governments have cut funding."

The emotion that had spasmed through him subsided, and he leaned back.

"I did things that were wrong. Things that were then and are now illegal. I am not denying that. But I want to emphasise two things for you. First, our intentions were good." One of the beads of sweat broke free and rolled down the side of his face. "Second, this was my idea, and my illegal scheme should not tarnish the reputation of this fine company and the outstanding people who work here. BMI is dropping all charges against Luke Smith, Victoria Headley and Silverthorne Staley Insurance Mergers and Acquisitions. Thank you for your attention and understanding."

A lawyer would have said Braun missed the perfect chance to express remorse. His triumphalism struck a sour note.

Most thought he'd lied. He had lied back then and he was lying now. Braun had siphoned off money, laundered it and hidden it. Sure, maybe a token amount went to medical research because it was good for his ego, but it was laughable that Braun-the-Brain Dieter-Make-Loadsa-Money gave 100% away. Good Samaritans don't hire a hitman. "Tell me another one," they said to each other, "pull the other leg." The people who had worked for him were particularly excoriating as they regaled each other with stories of Braun's heartlessness.

But there was the occasional person who saw the compassion he was capable of, on display for the first time. And recognised that he was a man who struggled with his own feelings, who had buried them to get the job done. And there was compassion for him in return.

— · —

The fasten seatbelts sign blinked back on. The announcement was soothing and boring. Due to a technical difficulty the plane would be touching down in Ireland for a short period to double check an inconsequential bit of kit and then the flight to Venezuela would resume.

After landing, the plane taxied and taxied from one runway to another to another before finally ending up near a large hanger. Men in blue uniforms were up the stairs almost before the plane had stopped. And they entered from both ends, meeting in first class.

The well-heeled looked on with consternation as they funnelled towards one immaculately dressed, good-looking businessman. He refused to go with them. He demanded to see the captain. He insisted he was a British citizen and could not be summarily evicted from a plane. It was outrageous, illegal, immoral and no, he wouldn't go.

In the end, the police had to physically bundle him off. His tongue went from protest to venom, which did not endear him to the police, and he then compounded the error by trying to buy them off. It was filmed. It was shared.

Fiona took a break from packing up her belongings to watch

it on her phone, and then passed the phone to Jane and Vicky. Fiona commented, "Braun ratted out Drinkwater to get himself a reduced sentence. That and his song-n-dance about saving AIDS victims."

"If Drinkwater had been cleverer, he'd have gone to the police first and beaten Braun to it," Jane added.

Watching it with an ear-to-ear grin was Vicky. "The only thing more perfect than Drinkwater being arrested was his hair."

CHAPTER 10:
Sunday

People were lined up to greet Luke as he entered the FT's studio with policemen and FT security staff behind him. There was a long line. He had been told they would virtually all be FT staff. Although they were all clearly conscious of the time constraint, the line moved quickly. Luke noticed that Vicky was right there, at the front, where she liked to be.

"This is our public reunion, and you are going to get a peck on the cheek," Vicky said. As he bent for the mutual cheek touch, she held his cheek against hers long enough to whisper, "Our private reunion is going to be a lot different from this."

His thoughts went to the night they had flirted, which seemed like another lifetime. A wave of emotion hit him, incoherent yet powerful. He could say nothing back.

"We are going to be live in a few minutes, people," was announced to the room. "Quiet please for the live interview with Luke Smith."

Luke tried to switch gears and compose himself for the Q&A.

"Good evening, my name is Khawla Khoury. I am the editor here at the Financial Times. You might know how the saga of Luke Smith began. And you have no doubt seen all the developments today, culminating in BMI's admission of wrongdoing and the dropping of charges against both Smith and the investment bank Silverthorne Staley." She turned her body slightly to face her guest. "Luke, tell us what happened between last

Friday and when you stormed into our building earlier today."

Luke was sitting behind a table, wearing a button-down blue shirt. He had shaved and was now sporting bandages on his face and hand. His left arm was in a sling.

"Thanks, Khawla. If you don't mind, I would like to begin by apologising once again to the people whose family and friends were in the database, and to all BMI policyholders for the anxiety this situation must have caused. I promise you that I protected the data as best I could.

"There's one more very important thing I want to reference before I go into the chain of events. As I will describe shortly, I used a turban and later a burqa to protect my identity. I realise those are very important items of religious clothing and I apologise if I caused any offence. It was strictly out of necessity because my safety was on the line.

"The timeline really starts late on Thursday, not on Friday. As part of the normal due diligence of the IPO, I was tasked with checking the actual death claims in BMI's source files against the numbers shown in the financials that investors would rely on. An extract from the claims file is all it would have taken to do this. It just happened that it was easier to send the whole file than to delay the process by making a smaller file. If the smaller file had been made and sent, this would not have been discovered. So it was a fluke that I ended up with the full file."

Luke described the medical emergency, how he'd found the turban, bought the camping gear, found the Polish Centre and Furnivall Gardens and started to analyse the data.

"Please tell us how you discovered the policies that paid into the Cayman Islands," Khawla asked.

"After I exhausted all of my own ideas, I used pattern recognition techniques that underly AI to find a relationship between parts of the data that the human eye might not catch."

"So, your human intelligence and Artificial Intelligence teamed up on this."

"Yes."

"Are there any questions from the audience?"

A lady in the audience put up her hand as though she was in school and Khawla nodded to her.

"In case you are not aware, there was a £100,000 reward on your head. Who do you think should get it?"

"I have thought about that actually. I'm not sure how the Polish Cultural Association is funded, but that would seem appropriate. The ability to just walk in there and to use their facilities was the most critical thing for me." He hesitated to make sure he chose his next words carefully. "I'm sure there are many deserving causes among the housing-challenged, but I came across a group of PTSD veterans camped out in Hyde Park before any of this started. Like all veterans everywhere, they've given a lot." He didn't want to go into the details of the chase. "How about half to them?"

In Hyde Park, Jocko blinked at the phone but was otherwise motionless as the yelling and movement started all around him. Softly to himself he said, "I knew that guy was legit the first time I met him."

"The last question, if I may," Khawla said, after glancing surreptitiously at the clock. "We know now that you basically camped in the middle of some bushes and slept under the stars, but I, and probably many others, just can't fathom how you were able to pull this off when thousands and thousands of us were looking for you."

"I was able to do that because London is a diverse and tolerant city. A city where someone wearing a turban or a burqa, or someone sleeping rough, can walk into a store or a library or grab a taxi. People are treated with respect and common decency regardless of their class, race, gender or colour. This is so precious and can't be taken for granted. That's how I was able to do this."

After a few seconds of absolute silence in the room, Khawla

ended the interview. She seemed a little surprised at its emphatic final note, but there was no doubt that was the point at which to end the show.

CHAPTER 11:
Monday

The queue at Heathrow was long and Sunday had ticked over into Monday. The passengers off the long-haul flight shuffled forwards. Unlike the others, the older Chinese couple was pulled aside by Customs and questioned. Then the Customs guard called his superior who called someone else. From a different room, a suit unfolded himself from a chair and briskly walked over.

"Hello," he said. "I'm Jason Zhou from the Home Office." He spoke perfect Cantonese. "Welcome to Great Britain. I am very sorry about what happened to your daughter, Amber. I have been sent to assist you in any way. Would you please come this way? We have a car waiting."

— . —

The reports on the gun from the suspect killed on Saturday had just come to McConley's inbox. McConley clicked it open and studied them. His Monday just got a whole lot better.

If there was ever a goldmine in law enforcement, McConley thought, *this was it.* The gun matched the ballistics for a dozen unsolved murders in the UK. And he had a rookie constable, Zofia Dabrowski, to thank.

He thought about it some more. *I have Luke Smith to thank for this too.*

EPILOGUE:
Three weeks later

It was actually more comfortable to stand than to sit. The stiff bandage from hip to knee made sitting in a chair a nuisance. Upright, crutches in her armpits, was actually not so bad.

Vicky Headley had come to visit her in the hospital. Her parents had quietly vacated the room and left them alone to talk. They'd both been a little bit in awe of each other and the conversation had started with the stilted awkward air of mutual appreciation.

"Amber, I'm so impressed that you didn't give up on that mortality issue. You found the same symptom that Luke found, you just didn't have the detailed file that he had to prove what they'd done."

"I was doing a course on data science at the time. That helped." Amber paused and then blurted out. "But I was certainly close to crossing the compliance line when I did all this."

Vicky gave a small snort of amusement. "Thank goodness your curiosity won out in the end. We're always looking for people who think critically and engage thoughtfully, using the full range of tools that we have at our disposal – and who don't give up. You did that. We'd be happy to have you work at Silverthorne. I would be your mentor."

Amber's eyes widened. There was a long silence. Vicky thought that Amber was weighing up her options and how much she could get paid.

But Amber surprised her when she said, "Drinkwater would have made a terrible boss. He could teach suffocation to a boa constrictor."

As witty one-liners, Amber didn't think it was half bad but Vicky didn't laugh. Instead she nodded sympathetically.

Amber tried again. "He travelled so far from right to wrong that he couldn't see them on a clear night with a telescope."

Again, not bad. Again Vicky smiled sympathetically.

Vicky heard what Amber wasn't saying. That she was mortified about the affair. That she knew she had misjudged. That she hoped the jokes would make it seem like the kind of things people did all the time: fuck corrupt married murderers who then try to kill you. You know, because adulting sucks.

But Vicky also heard the voice of the young – clever, hardworking and schooled – just green as a valley in Wales. Vicky finally replied, "You've already impressed me. Now you need to just be." It was a truth that Vicky had discovered only recently.

It was Amber's turn to be surprised. She hadn't a clue what that meant: just be. She tucked it away to think about later and said, "I was thinking. In hindsight, this BMI thing wasn't really that different than the Post Office disaster. Once Luke Smith had the data, even though he didn't know what he had, he got blamed. Like it was all his fault. Plus, the money siphoned off could have provided bigger dividends to policyholders, rather than being hidden in some off-shore account. Do you think anyone realises that Braun effectively took money out of the pockets of every policyholder, every widow and orphan?"

Vicky grinned. "If anyone says that aloud it's going to start an even bigger shitstorm."

"The only person who knew I was going to the actuarial eating club dinner was Drinkwater. But I never told him about my friend, Xiaowei Deng. What I told him instead was how I was crunching the stolen data file. I was bragging. In the beginning, he was super interested. Later, he only wanted to know where

I was, down to the exact address and time. Then the police-woman phoned and told me that my life was in danger. Once he showed up in the classroom I put it together. Then I knew he was dangerous, but I didn't want anyone else hurt so I did as he told me to. To protect the others."

Vicky nodded again, adding quite forcefully, "No one's going to blame you for misjudging Alaistair Drinkwater. You're far from the only person who did so. More to the point, you showed resilience, real strength of character. What's the buzz word nowadays? Grit. You got grit."

A smile broke out on Amber's troubled face. And relief. Tears gathered in her eyes. She'd never thought of herself as having grit. She'd always thought of herself as just being lonely.

"I would very much like to come to Silverthorne and work for you, Vicky."

Vicky smiled back at her. "Excellent. I'll put together a new pay package for you."

"As an example of my grit, could I please ask if there could be time for me to play rugby, once I'm all healed up?"

"That can absolutely be accommodated. There's room for a work-life balance these days, even at Silverthorne."

— · —

Zofia slept in for half an hour that morning. Knowing she was working from home made her feel better – not just mentally but physically as well. When she looked back at her deductions on the Luke Smith case, she was both amused and appalled that every single one had been comprehensively wrong. She had stood in the tracks of both Luke Smith and the killer at the Polish Centre. Plus, the AI tools had bailed her out. Her shining moment of glory, her little bit of pride, was chasing the guy and pulling the trigger.

In short, the experience had humbled her.

She and Maria reported directly to McConley now, tasked with making sure all the traditional blokes in the Met and MI5 knew how to use the new AI tools. She hoped to God that she would do him and Petr and the baby proud, and more crimes would be solved as a result. In five minutes, she would be starting the first virtual training session. She had everyone's undivided attention now, and she wanted to take full advantage.

The door cracked open, and Petr peeked in. Hearing no conversation and seeing her screen wasn't on, he entered and kissed the top of her head from behind, one hand on her shoulder, the other on the bump.

— · —

"So, what's next for you, Miss Headley?" Luke whispered into Vicky's ear the next morning.

"Silverthorne was quick to welcome me back, even gave me some time off to go back home and chill with my family. They explicitly said I was still on a partnership track."

"That's great. You deserve all of those things."

She sat up in the bed and looked down at him. "How is your family after all this? It must have been awful for them."

"It was. It was very helpful that I was able to go straight back and be with them in person. Helpful for me too. To be able to reflect a bit on everything."

"Anything to share from that reflection?"

"The reality is that, after all this, my working and earning career are over. Now that I can look backwards at it, it looks different. I worked hard going through all that specific professional training and following that road down a scripted, high-stress career. In today's terms, I followed the algorithm."

Vicky nodded, knowing exactly what he meant.

"And I didn't just submit to the algorithm, I helped to build that road, with publications and presentations. Like a good insurance guy, I made a living out of putting people into buckets based on numbers, stuff like that. But this jolted me off that road and out of my comfort zone. A new physical environment, new friends and enemies. And that didn't come easily to me."

He didn't want to say the next part aloud and overrode the engrained habit of always appearing as if the world was his oyster. "It sure dented my confidence." He paused. And then insisted on reaching for a deeper and darker truth. "No, it crushed my confidence. It changed me." He was groping to put into words a feeling. "Now that I'm off the road, I think I want to stay off. What that means specifically, I'm not sure."

There was silence as they both got out of bed and prepared for the day. He expected that she was thinking something very similar to him. Building a lasting intimate relationship would probably be hard. He tried to picture Vicky outside London. And couldn't. Would he get to meet Vicky's friends? Her family? Would they be flying back together? They were both at personal turning points. Hopefully on the same journey.

"I'll bet you didn't have to study English poetry in school?" she asked.

"Safe bet," he replied.

"I got very bored while you were off hiding in bushes and got my books out. Found one thing that stuck. Keats. I think he wrote this for us. *Do you not see how necessary a world of pains and troubles is to school an intelligence and make it a soul?*"

Their deepening thoughts were interrupted by the alarm on the nightstand. They turned to look at it in surprise. He smiled and kissed her forehead as she tried to turn it off.

"You have a staff meeting or something?" he asked. "Maybe it's a performance review?"

She blushed, then squinted her eyes and went with his thought "Okay, for strategy, you already have an A+ for the single rose, and another A+ for renting this houseboat. You've got nowhere to go but down, buddy." And glanced south. Then raised an eyebrow at him.

Luke burst into laughter. He really enjoyed her wicked sense of humour.

"And on the execution side," she said, grinning and blushing even more, "I'm going to need to collect a lot more data before I have a statistically valid assessment."

The alarm went off again, and her look changed to frustration as she tried to turn it off, this time permanently. He took it from her hands. The damn thing was programmed with some kind of data chip. Neither of them could figure it out. The ringing was insistent. Luke strode to the door of the houseboat and flung the hatch back. With an easy arc of his arm, he tossed the alarm clock high in the air. There was a splash and then a sudden silence.

They both burst into laughter. "That's one way to deal with a faulty system," Vicky commented dryly.

"Now what?" asked Luke.

"The Dove. This time you can actually go inside and have a drink, for a change."

ABOUT THE AUTHOR

 Mark W. Griffin, debut author of *The Mortality Thief*, is a Chartered Financial Analyst, actuary and EMT. Working as a Chief Risk Officer, he has been responsible for not just a lot of analysis, but telling stories about what has gone wrong, what could go wrong, and serving as the corporate incarnation of cop, investigator, and crime reporter.

He is passionate about ice hockey, and just about any outdoor activity, particularly uphill skiing. He has split his career between the UK, the US, and Canada. He lives in New York State with his family and their rescue dog Ollie.